DEATHBOAT DELUXE

I was enjoying my walk on deck with Mary Ward, the lady from North Carolina who had won a trip on the *QE2* for winning a contest in mystery solving. We were both reveling in the brisk breeze and the sea-scented air.

"You know, Mary," I said, "this *is* bracing."

She'd moved from my side and didn't answer. She was leaning forward over a lifeboat, as though to better see something.

"What is it?" I asked, joining her.

I didn't need an answer because I saw what she had seen—a woman's bare foot poking up through a small gap in the orange tarp. As shocking as it was, my focus for the first few seconds was on the perfectly applied nail polish on her toes, which was only to be expected from one of the passengers on this supership where everything was done in style. Even murder . . .

MURDER ON THE *QE2*

A *Murder, She Wrote* Mystery

A Novel by Jessica Fletcher
and Donald Bain
based on the
Universal television series
created by Peter S. Fischer,
Richard Levinson & William Link

A SIGNET BOOK

SIGNET
Published by the Penguin Group
Penguin Putnam Inc., 375 Hudson Street
New York, New York 10014, U.S.A.
Penguin Books Ltd. 27 Wrights Lane
London W8 5TZ, England
Penguin Books Australia Ltd, Ringwood,
Victoria, Australia
Penguin Books Canada Ltd, 10 Alcorn Avenue,
Toronto, Ontario, Canada M4V 3B2
Penguin Books (N.Z.) Ltd, 182–190 Wairau Road,
Auckland 10, New Zealand

Penguin Books Ltd, Registered Offices:
Harmondsworth, Middlesex, England

First published by Signet, an imprint of Dutton Signet,
a member of Penguin Putnam Inc.

First Printing, October, 1997
10 9 8 7 6 5 4 3 2 1

PUBLISHER'S NOTE
This is a work of fiction. Names, characters, places, and incidents either are
the product of the author's imagination or are used fictitiously, and any
resemblance to actual persons, living or dead, events, or locales is entirely
coincidental.

Chapter One

The older I get, the harder it is to surprise me.

But when Matt Miller, my literary agent, called late last winter from New York with a new and unusual project for me, I was surprised to the point of near-shock.

"I can't believe this," I said. "Why *me*?"

"The fact that you're the world's most successful and best-known mystery writer is reason enough, Jess." He laughed. "I've delivered lots of good news to you, but I've never heard you so excited before. As I said, it doesn't pay that much, and it means having to drop the book you're working on for a month, but—"

"Matt," I said, "one day soon I'll explain why I'm so enthusiastic. In the meantime, I'm running late for lunch with Seth Hazlitt. You remember him."

"Sure. Cabot Cove's answer to Marcus Welby. Say hello for me."

"I certainly will. Can I call you later for more details?"

"I'll be here all day."

I hung up and let out a loud yelp of joy.

But that euphoria lasted only a few minutes, replaced by a wave of sadness.

It was twenty years ago that I made my first, and only transatlantic crossing on the fabled *Queen Elizabeth Two—QE2*—the grande dame of all ocean liners. My husband, Frank, was alive then, and had given me—us—the crossing as a joint Christmas present.

We set sail on May twenty-eighth of that year and reveled in the ship's majesty, and the pampering we received from its large international staff. It was the most pleasurable five days of my life. But it involved far more than the wonderful, seemingly unlimited gourmet food, tea dances at four each afternoon, movies and lively shows and the pool and spa, the dance classes and endless Champagne parties, or being wrapped in a blanket on the top deck at eleven in the morning and served hot bouillon by a courteous young steward.

What was especially memorable was to stand on the deck in fog and heaving seas, and to sense the adventure of being where Columbus and other fearless explorers had gone before without the advantage of advanced navigation technology, or knowing there was a port just a few days away.

My recollection of that trip was as clear as though I'd taken it yesterday.

Frank and I stood on the *QE2*'s Helicopter Deck, its highest, arms about each other, peering into the distance at Southampton, England, after five glorious days at sea.

"Know what I think, Jess?" he said.

"No. What?"

"I think we should make this a yearly event. Save toward it all year. Treat ourselves to this grand experience every May we're alive and can enjoy it together."

I hugged him tighter. "For a conservative New Englander, Frank, you do have your extravagant moments."

"Of course I do," he said. "But only when it concerns you."

We kissed, and spent the next week in London extending the moment.

We never sailed across the North Atlantic again. Frank became very ill shortly after we returned home, and died later that year. Of course, I often thought about making another crossing on the *QE2*, especially when May twenty-eighth rolled around. But I could never bring myself to call Susan Shevlin, my travel agent in Cabot Cove, and book myself a stateroom. I just didn't want to do it without Frank.

But this was different.

This was business.

"Say again, Jessica?" Dr. Seth Hazlitt said at lunch. We'd been best of friends for more years than I care to admit.

"They want me to lecture about writing murder mysteries, on the *QE2* between New York and Southampton. I'll be one of a group of people lecturing on different subjects. And I'm to write a murder mystery play to be acted by a Los Angeles theatrical troupe."

"Sounds like a fairly good thing," he said in his usual understated way. "How do you feel about travelin' alone?"

"I hadn't thought about it, Seth. I travel alone all the time."

"But not on a big ship crossin' the Atlantic Ocean."

"What difference does that make?"

"Makes a considerable difference, it seems to me. I could go along with you."

"That would be lovely, Seth, but—"

"We'll talk more about it. In the meantime, finish your lobster roll, Jessica. Especially good, wouldn't you say?"

"Yes, Seth. It's especially good."

I called Matt Miller the moment I returned home. He'd been one of advertising's top commercial directors, and I'd met him when he directed me in a twenty-second public service announcement. After a stint as president of the Association of Independent Commercial Producers, he decided to follow his natural love of books and became a literary agent, my literary agent and one of the best in the business.

"So, Matt, tell me more about this intriguing assignment."

"Okay," he said. "I talked to the director of ship-board entertainment and made some notes. Let's see. You'll be one of a half dozen speakers. Not much of a commitment. Two one-hour talks in the afternoon, on the second and fourth days at sea. And, of course, you have to write an original murder mystery for the actors to perform."

"How long a play?" I asked.

"Two hours. They'll perform it over four days, so it has to be four short acts. I have the name and number of the director. Name's Nestor. He's in Los Angeles, although I understand he'll use actors from New York. You should give him a call." He rattled off the information, which I wrote down.

"I know I'll have free passage because of the lectures. But writing an original play is another thing."

Miller laughed. "It's about time you started thinking about money, Jess. Don't worry. I'll make sure you're more than adequately compensated."

"I wasn't worried," I said. "Any idea who the other lecturers will be?"

"As a matter of fact, I do. Let's see. There's Marla Tralaine. She'll be speaking."

"Marla Tralaine? The actress?"

"One and the same."

"I know this sounds callous, Matt, but I wasn't even sure she was still alive. I haven't read or heard any-thing about her in ages."

"I know. After that sordid episode with her fourth

husband—or was it her fifth?—and she had those back-to-back box office bombs, her career dropped dead. Just the career. Not the woman. She's alive and well, I understand. Is even shopping a book proposal around town, and is negotiating to do a made-for-TV movie as her comeback vehicle. At any rate, she'll be one of your fellow lecturers."

"I'd forgotten about that business with her husband. They tried to pin his murder on her, as I recall."

"That's right. But they couldn't prove it."

"Well, I look forward to meeting her. Who else?"

"Ever watch Carlo Di Giovanni's cooking show?"

"Sometimes."

"Ever try one of his recipes?"

"No. But I enjoy him. He's funny. Very volatile. Very . . . Italian."

"He'll do some cooking as part of his lecture. You'll come away a five-star pasta chef."

"Wonderful."

"Troy Radcliff will be on board."

"Who's he?"

"A mountain climber. Set the world's record. He's pretty old now. Must be in his eighties."

"I don't follow mountain climbing."

"Which pleases me. Hate to lose my favorite client to a rock slide."

"No fear of that," I said.

"Radcliff hosts *Go For It*, the TV adventure show."

"Haven't seen that."

"Just as well. Finally, there's Elaine Ananthous, and—"

"She writes all those gardening books," I said.

"And, she is my client. You'll like Elaine. A little quirky, but nice. And Dan Solon has signed on for the cruise."

"Crossing," I said. "They never call it a cruise."

"I stand corrected."

"Who is Dan Solon?"

"The judge who presided over the K.C. James murder trial."

"Oh. *That* Dan Solon."

"He's writing a book, too, about the trial. Just started his own TV talk show. That's about it, Jess. An august group, wouldn't you say?"

"An eclectic one, Matt. Sounds like fun."

"Good. I suggest you get hold of the director as soon as possible."

"I'll call him when I ring off with you. Writing a play. I haven't done that in years. Should be a challenge."

"One I'm sure you'll face head-on, and successfully."

"By the way, when is the crossing?"

"You have lots of time. Three months."

"Oh?"

"You sail from New York on May twenty-eighth."

13

Chapter Two

"Mr. Nestor, please," I said to the woman who answered the phone at Nestor Productions in Los Angeles.

"Hey, Rip," I heard her yell. "It's for you."

A moment later, Mr. Nestor came on the line. "Rip Nestor here. This is Jessica Fletcher?"

"Yes, it is. My agent, Matt Miller, suggested I call you regarding the play on the QE2."

"Right. Yeah. Looking forward to a script from the famous Jessica Fletcher. When can I have it?"

"The script?" I laughed. "I'm afraid I need some input from you before I even consider doing it."

"What do you need to know from me?"

"Well, I . . . I'd like to know the sort of mystery plays you put on. Are they . . . are they broad and farcical? Slapstick? Cozy mysteries? Intellectual? Is there audience participation? I saw a dinner theater production years ago at a local Holiday Inn. I don't remember much of it, but as I recall, it was played very expansively. Lots of humor, and the audience got involved."

"You've got it. That's it. Entertain the audience. Keep 'em laughing. Get 'em to take part, become suspects, be questioned by the police. That sort of thing."

"I see. Mr. Nestor, could you tell me if—?"

"Call me Rip."

"Rip. Yes. Well, Rip, could you tell me how long a play you want?"

"The *QE2* show? Four half-hour acts. Big climax at the end of each. You know. Somebody killed."

"That's a lot of murders," I said.

"The more the better." His laugh was a cackle.

"All right," I said. "Will I have a chance to meet you in the near future?"

"I'll be in New York next week."

"Next week? I have to be there, too, for a few days, to meet with my publisher. Maybe we can find some time together."

"That'd be cool. I'll be staying at the Waldorf."

We exchanged information—I'd be staying at a Manhattan hotel that's a particular favorite of mine, the Sheraton-Park Avenue at Park and Thirty-seventh, a small, European-style jewel of a place that makes me feel at home. We made a tentative lunch date; he would call me at the hotel the day I arrived.

After we concluded our telephone conversation, I tried to get back to work on my latest novel, but found it hard to concentrate. My mind kept drifting back to memories of the *QE2*, of Frank, and of the reality I'd be back on that splendid ship in a few months.

Which meant shifting mental gears in order to put together not only two lectures, but a two-hour play as well. Should I base the play on one of my earlier murder mysteries? That was a possibility. But I wasn't sure I had the legal right to adapt one of my books for the stage without my publisher becoming legally involved. No. Better to come up with an original creation, written specifically to be performed.

The phone rang. It was my friend and Cabot Cove's sheriff, Morton Metzger.

"Afternoon, Mrs. F.," he said.

"Good afternoon, Mort. How are you this fine day?"

"Tip-top. Had to chase a crazy tourist speedin' through town a few hours ago. Finally pulled him over and he whips out his wallet and tries to bribe me."

"That's terrible."

"*Ayuh.* He tells me he knows how cops in little towns don't get paid much, so he figures I could use an extra twenty."

I couldn't help but smile as I envisioned the scene.

"I told him he was right, that I don't get paid what I'm worth, and that an extra twenty would come in right handy."

"And?"

"He grinned. A dumb, big grin, which didn't last once I told him he was under arrest for speedin', reckless endangerment, and attempting to bribe an officer of the law. Slapped the cuffs on him and took him down to the jail, where he is as we speak."

"Bravo!" I said.

"Thought you'd get a chuckle out 'a that, Mrs. F. Now, what's this I hear about you takin' a cruise on the *Queen Elizabeth 2*?"

"It's not a cruise, Mort. It's a crossing. The North Atlantic, unless bad weather causes the captain to choose a more southerly route." I remembered that from when Frank and I made the crossing.

"Sure you want to do it?" he asked.

"Why wouldn't I, for heaven's sake?"

"Well, Seth told me about it, and he thinks—"

Of course. Mort's concern was really Seth Hazlitt talking.

"Mort," I said, "I am thrilled at the chance to sail on the *QE2* again. I can't wait. Did Seth tell you I'll be writing an original murder mystery play, to be performed onboard?"

"*Ayuh*, that he did."

"Isn't that wonderful, Mort?"

"Frankly, Mrs. F., that's really the point of why I called."

"What is the point, Mort?"

"Well, you know how I invented that murder mystery board game, and almost sold it to Parker Brothers?"

"Yes."

"About a year ago I decided to write a play based on that same board game."

"Oh?"

"Yup. I did. And I was wondering whether you might want to use it on your cruise."

"Crossing."

"Crossing. Seth said you're writing a play for some director out in Hollywood."

"That's right."

"Well, I figured you might show my play to him, suggest he buy it. With your fame and influence, Mrs. F., he should listen up to you."

I didn't know what to say.

"Mrs. F.?"

"I'm here, Mort."

"How about it? We could share the money. Royalties, they call it. Right?"

"Right. Mort, I'll be happy to read your play."

"I'll head over with it right now. Always keep a copy in the car, just in case."

"Just in case? Of course. I understand. I'll be here. But Mort, I can't promise to submit it to the director. They're paying *me* to write the play."

"I know, I know, Mrs. F., but maybe—"

"I look forward to seeing it," I said.

I'd no sooner hung up, and had gone to the kitchen to make myself a cup of tea, when the phone rang again.

"Hello?" I said into my kitchen extension.

"Jessica?"

"Charlene?"

"Yes. How are you?"

"Just fine. You?"

"Great."

Charlene Sassi owns Cabot Cove's best bakery. She's a world-class cook and a friend.

"Jess, I just heard about your cruise on the *QE2*, and that you're writing a play for it."

Amazing, I thought, how efficient the Cabot Cove grapevine was. It's more effective than the Internet and World Wide Web combined.

"It's a crossing, Charlene. They call it a crossing."

"Of course they do," she said, laughing loudly. "That's because it's a . . . crossing . . . not a cruise. I knew that."

"What can I do for you?"

"Do you remember my brother's oldest boy?"

"No."

"His name is John. He goes to the U of Maine at Orono."

"Uh-huh."

"He wants to be a writer. Plays."

"Oh?"

"And he's written an original murder mystery. I bet he was inspired by you."

"That's very flattering, Charlene."

"Well, when I heard there was going to be a professional acting group from Hollywood on the cruise . . . the crossing . . . I immediately thought you might want to submit John's play to the director. It's so hard for a young person to reach big-time directors, as you well know."

"Yes, it is," I said. I went on to explain that the director, Rip Nestor—was he a big-time director?—I doubted it—wanted *me* to write the play.

There was a stony silence on the other end.

"But I'd love to read John's play," I quickly added.

"You would?"

"Absolutely," I said.

After hanging up, I realized I'd committed to reading two plays, without even having begun writing my own. Not being able to say no is a curse I share with many writer friends. Reading other people's work is time-consuming, especially if you take it seriously and want to offer constructive editing and advice.

Oh, well. I'd find the time.

I always do.

Chapter Three

It had snowed in New York the day before I flew there from Cabot Cove for two days of meetings. But the sun was shining brightly as Jed Richardson, owner, operator, and only pilot for Jed's Flying Service, landed smoothly at La Guardia Airport in one of his three aircraft, a single-engine Cessna. Jed decided to stick around New York until it was time for me to fly back, so we shared a taxi into the city and checked into the hotel before going our separate ways.

Rip Nestor insisted we have lunch at a Manhattan sushi restaurant. I am not particularly fond of raw fish, no matter how beautifully it's presented. Unless, of course, it's shellfish served as part of a classic New England clambake. But I didn't protest. Every sushi restaurant I've been to offers other choices for customers with a pedestrian palate, like me.

Mr. Nestor was, I judged, in his early thirties. He was tall and slender, with reddish hair pulled tight from front to back across the top of his head, and down into a long ponytail. He wore tight jeans, laced-up ankle-high work boots, a green T-shirt with NESTOR PRODUCTIONS emblazoned in white across the chest, and a tan safari jacket. Multiple gold chains of varying lengths, large sunglasses, and an expensive leather shoulder bag completed the Hollywood picture.

"Good trip?" I asked after we'd been seated.

"The red-eye," he said, yawning to make the point. "How do you get here from Maine?"

"We actually have an airport in Cabot Cove," I said.

He smiled. "I didn't mean—"

"A good friend flew me here," I said. "He runs a small air service out of Cabot Cove. A small, single-engine plane. But convenient. He was a top-rated airline pilot for years."

"How's the script coming?" Nestor asked, picking up a menu and lifting his sunglasses in order to read it.

"I told you I wouldn't start on it until we had this opportunity to talk."

"Sushi? The combination platter?" he asked, returning menu and sunglasses to their previous positions.

"I see they have tempura," I said. "I'll have that."

"Cholesterol city," he said.

I ignored the comment, and we ordered. I asked, "Do you specialize in producing and directing murder mystery plays, Mr. Nestor?"

"Call me Rip, please."

I always have trouble calling people Chuck, or Buck, or Rock, and now Rip. But I did. "All right, Rip," I said.

"Do murder mysteries constitute the bulk of your work?"

"No," he said. "I do a lot of low-budget films. A couple of made-for-TV shows. But interactive mysteries are very popular these days. V-e-r-y popular. So I set up Malibu Mysteries. We do dinner theater up and down the state."

"Interesting," I said. "Do you work ships very often?"

"More and more. But this is my first on the *QE2*. You ever been on it?"

"Yes. Years ago. I was with—" I felt a lump developing in my throat and changed the subject. "So, Rip, tell me what you want in this script I'm to write."

"I really prefer to leave that to you, Mrs. Fletcher."

"It's Jessica."

"Right. It's your call, Jessica. Actually, I have a dozen, maybe more, standard plays we use. Different styles, different approaches to match up with whatever audience books us. We do a lot of corporate work. Conventions."

"I see."

"But the entertainment director for Cunard decided since you were going to be on board anyway giving a lecture, it would be good marketing to have you write an original play. I assume they'll advertise it a lot. Makes sense."

"I suppose it does. I still wish you could give me a better idea of the sort of play you'd like me to write."

He responded by pulling videotapes from his bag

and handing them to me. "These are two of our most popular shows. I wasn't going to give them to you because I didn't want to influence what you write. But they'll give you an idea of how I work."

"Thanks," I said, putting the tapes in my bag.

"Actually," he said, "I do have an idea on how to make this show different. You know, special—aside from it being written by the world's most famous mystery writer."

"I'm hardly that," I said.

"You're too modest. Cunard's entertainment director gave me the names of the other lecturers who'll be on board. Quite a list. Troy Radcliff, the mountain climber. The TV chef, Di Giovanni, and that strange lady who talks to plants and flowers. Oh, and the judge from the K.C. James trial."

"Judge Solon."

"Right. And that bitch, Marla Tralaine."

"Oh?"

He shrugged. "Pardon my French. Anyway, I was thinking that maybe you could write them into the script. Just walk-on parts, a line or two. Could be fun weaving their areas of expertise into the show."

"An interesting idea," I said. "Of course, it will depend upon whether they're willing to take part."

"I'm sure you could persuade them."

"Me? Maybe the entertainment director should be the one."

"Whatever works," he said. "Enjoy your tempura?"

"Yes. It was excellent."

"Hate to eat and run, Jessica, but I have another appointment."

"And so do I."

Since he didn't reach for the check, I did, paid it, and we said good-bye on the sidewalk.

"You'll have it to me in a month?" he said, referring to the promise I'd made during lunch to deliver the script in thirty days.

"Yes," I said.

"Just one last thing," he said.

"Which is?"

"Keep the cast small. There's a budget."

"I'm glad you mentioned it, although having all the other lecturers take part hardly accomplishes that."

"I mean the professional cast, the actors and actresses, the ones I have to pay. I figure the lecturers will do it for fun."

I wasn't sure he was right, but didn't wish to debate it.

"*Ciao*, Mrs. Fletcher," he said. "Thanks for lunch."

Chapter Four

Having the script to write helped pass what turned out to be an especially cold and snowy late February and early March. It took me a number of false starts before I could really get into the story. One of the problems was working in a format that was alien to me.

The last time I'd attempted to write a script was for a television adaptation of one of my novels. I was pleased with the result; the producer said he was, too.

I knew that television shows and motion pictures were collaborative efforts, with the original writer's work subject to rewrite by committee. But what appeared on the screen bore virtually no resemblance to what I'd written. It was demoralizing, of course, but I quickly got over it and went on to other things.

The two videos given me by Rip Nestor proved helpful, but off-putting. If they were indicative of what he expected from me, I knew I was in for a month-long struggle. The scripts and performances were broad to the point of farce, the interaction with the audiences spirited and loud. After watching them, I knew I could never write that way. Mr. Nestor would have to be content with Jessica Fletcher's style.

Although I'd agreed to contact personally the other lecturers scheduled to sail with me in May to see whether they'd be willing to take parts in the play, I decided not to. I wrote the play in such a way that if any one of them, or more, declined to participate, it was easy to adapt the script on the spot to cover their absence.

But I did watch their TV shows. I found it interesting that they all appeared on the same cable network, the Teller Network, a new addition to Cabot Cove's cable service's array of programs. The network's owner, Sam Teller, was a controversial person in broadcasting. His reputation, at least what I'd read in the papers, was that of a rich, ruthless businessman whose list of enemies was long and distinguished. He was married to a young actress named Lila Sims; their names appeared in the gossip columns and on tabloid TV with regularity.

I also stayed up late one night to watch Marla Tralaine in one of her earlier films, *Dangerous Woman*. She was stunningly beautiful, although I had to agree with critics that her acting range was limited and one-dimensional. But who was I to judge? I'm a writer, not an actress. In the film she played a classic femme fatale, the proverbial "other woman" who gets it in the end.

Prompted by seeing Marla Tralaine on-screen, I

went to my local library and pulled up a few old newspaper articles about her husband's murder, and her being charged with the crime. It made for interesting reading. At least I knew something about this woman who would be one of my companions on the *QE2* for five days.

I proudly typed THE END on the script and sent it by Federal Express to Rip Nestor in Los Angeles. Feeling refreshingly liberated, at least until I got back to the book I'd shelved, I ventured out from my self-imposed hibernation to touch base again with Cabot Cove friends.

"Well, what do you think, Mrs. F.?" Sheriff Mort Metzger asked me as we had breakfast with Seth Hazlitt in Mara's luncheonette. An unusually early spring thaw had set in; sunlight streamed through the window into our booth and onto plates piled high with blueberry pancakes.

"About what?" I asked.

"My play."

"Oh, Mort, I meant to mention that. I didn't want to start reading it until I finished writing my own because I was afraid it would . . . influence me."

Mort looked dejected.

"But it's the first thing on my agenda today," I said brightly.

"I was hopin' you'd send it to your director friend in Hollywood," Mort said, "instead of having to write one yourself."

"And I still may," I said. "Mr. Nestor has a catalogue of mystery plays he uses, depending upon which audience is involved. Maybe he'll add your play to his repertoire."

"You think he will?" Mort asked.

"We'll keep our fingers crossed."

We all looked up as Charlene Sassi entered the luncheonette and came to our booth.

"Morning, Charlene," Seth said, his corpulent midsection wedged against the table, keeping him from standing.

"Good morning everyone," she said, sliding in next to Mort.

"Morning rush over?" Seth asked our favorite baker.

"Yes," Charlene said, exhaling with gusto. "Ran out of donuts. That hasn't happened in a long time. Must be the break in the weather." She looked at me. "So, Jess, will my nephew be the next Neil Simon?"

"To be honest with you, Charlene, I haven't had a chance to read John's play. I've been so busy writing my own that—"

"What play?" Mort asked.

Charlene explained.

Mort's expression was one of abject despair.

"Mort," I said, "I'm perfectly capable of reading two plays." I placed my hand on his.

"But Charlene's nephew goes to college," Mort said. "He's educated in writing. You'll like his a lot better than mine."

"Well, we'll just see," I said. "These pancakes are delicious."

As always happens, reading the two scripts given me by my friends took much longer than I'd anticipated. I made pages of notes suggesting editorial changes, although I constantly acknowledged that I was not a playwright, and so my reactions should be judged with that in mind.

I delivered the scripts back to them, then settled in to finish my novel. It was difficult because my thoughts kept wandering to the contemplation of May twenty-eighth when I would board the *QE2* for the second time in my life. But I played all sorts of mind games to keep my thoughts and energies channeled, and managed to finish the book on May twenty-second.

It took a long time for Rip Nestor to react to the script I'd sent him. He called in late April to tell me he loved it, and that he was in the process of putting together a cast for the May twenty-eighth crossing. His call boosted my spirits, which had been flagging. Writers work alone, in a vacuum, with a lack of frequent and ongoing feedback to their creative efforts. I've always felt that every publisher should have someone on staff whose only job is to call writers under contract, ask how things are going, and give them a feeling that someone else cares about their work. It will never happen, but it would be nice if it did.

Susan Shevlin, my travel agent, gave me all sorts of

promotional material about Cunard and the *QE2*, and a handsome portfolio arrived in the mail. It contained everything I needed to know about life aboard the massive ocean-going vessel. The middle three nights of the five nights at sea would be formal. There was a three-dimensional cutaway map of the ship; it was like a small city. A "dictionary" of nautical terms briefed me on the difference between port and starboard. I was told how I could receive and send telephone and fax messages from the ship, using satellite communications. And every shipboard amenity, including the beauty shop and spa, the casino, bars and cocktail lounges (there were nine), dining rooms, computer learning center, library, bookstore, entertainment, gift shops (including a branch of London's famed Harrods), florist, hospital and medical staff, valet and laundry services, was explained. There was a kennel for pets and a day-care center for little children.

As I said, the *QE2* is a floating city.

The portfolio also contained my boarding pass and cabin assignment. I would be staying in Cabin Number 1037, which meant I would take my meals in the Queens Grill, one of five restaurants. I had a spark of déjà vu; Frank and I had enjoyed the ambiance of the Queens Grill level of accommodations when we sailed twenty years ago.

What to wear, what to wear?

I gathered a few of my female friends from Cabot Cove to help me decide on a wardrobe. It turned into a wonderful party, with lots of laughter and good-natured kidding of me and my clothing dilemma. After modeling myriad choices for them, a consensus was reached, and the clothes I would pack were decided.

On May twenty-seventh, the night before I was to leave, these same female friends, augmented by my male buddies, including Seth Hazlitt, Sheriff Mort Metzger, Susan Shevlin's husband, Jim, the mayor of Cabot Cove, and others, threw me a bon voyage party at Cabot Cove's newest restaurant, Simone's, owned by a large Italian family who also operated a popular pizza parlor. The mood was festive, the food classic peasant Italian fare: pasta to start, veal spiced and cooked to perfection, and a rolling dessert cart that should have come with a gift certificate to a spa.

We said our good-byes outside the restaurant. I was tired; I had to be up early for my flight to New York with Jed Richardson. The *QE2* would set sail between three and four in the afternoon. I was advised to be at the dock by two.

"Well, Jessica," said Seth Hazlitt, "all I can say is that I wish you a safe and smooth passage."

"Thank you, Seth." I kissed him on the cheek.

"Stay away from that midnight buffet," Jim Shevlin said. "If you don't, you won't fit in Jed's small plane for the trip home."

"Don't worry about that," I said. "I intend to exercise discipline for the five days."

"Sure," Charlene Sassi chimed in. "Until you get a

taste of all that scrumptious food, morning, noon, and night."

"Pack that seasick medicine I gave you?" Seth asked.

"I certainly did, along with the wristbands and patches. But I don't intend to get sick. I never do."

"Always a first time," Seth said grimly. "If none of those things work, you get right down to see the ship's doctor, get a shot."

Eventually, my friends ran out of advice, and I made it home, where I put the finishing touches on my packing. I was about to get into bed at midnight when the phone rang.

"Jessica?"

"Yes?"

"Matt Miller."

"Oh, hi, Matt."

"Sorry to call so late, but I wanted to say two things."

"Happy to hear them."

"First of all, I read the novel. It's wonderful. One of your best efforts. I couldn't put it down."

"That's great to hear."

"And two, I wanted to wish you an absolutely wonderful cruise."

"Actually, it's a crossing. Not a cruise."

"Then I wish you an absolutely wonderful crossing."

"Thank you. I intend to revel in every moment of it. Between the latest novel and the script, I've had quite enough of murder to last a good long time. I need five days of utter peace and calm."

"Then that's what you shall have, Jess. Enjoy!"

"I'll call you when I'm back."

I didn't sleep a wink.

Chapter Five

"Mrs. Fletcher."

I'd just gotten out of a taxi that had brought me from La Guardia Airport to the pier at Manhattan's Twelfth Avenue, where the QE2 sat majestically awaiting its passengers. The ship is an awesome sight, its red-and-black funnel rising proudly into the sky, its sparkling navy hull, almost a thousand feet long and more than a hundred feet wide, dazzling the eye.

I turned to the voice that had called my name. It belonged to a pretty, smiling young blond woman wearing a blue blazer over her white blouse, the Cunard name and symbol emblazoned on its breast pocket.

"Yes?" I said as my driver unloaded my luggage from the cab's trunk.

"Hi. I'm Priscilla Warren. I'll be your Cunard escort on the crossing."

"Pleased to meet you, Ms. Warren."

"Please call me Priscilla. Or Pris, if you prefer. I figured I'd stand out here instead of waiting at the check-in desk. I've read most of your books, and have seen your picture dozens of times. Recognized you right away."

"I'm glad." I looked around. "My goodness," I said, "quite a mob scene."

Ms. Warren laughed, which she did easily and often. "We're sold out, Mrs. Fletcher. A full house."

"That's good for your company," I said.

She waved over a man with a hand truck, who loaded my bags onto it. I'd tagged them with precoded luggage tags contained in the material I'd been sent. An efficient system.

I followed Priscilla into the cavernous terminal, where hundreds of people milled about waiting to board. "Good flight from home?" she asked as we walked.

"Oh, yes." I explained that I'd been flown to La Guardia from Maine by my pilot friend, Jed Richardson.

"That's the way to travel," she said.

"I wish he could pick me up when I come back from London," I said. "But he's committed elsewhere. I'll be taking the Delta Shuttle to Boston."

"If there's anything I can do to help," Priscilla said, "just let me know. That's what I'm here for."

We stopped at a desk, behind which stood three Cunard employees. "Hey, guys, this is Jessica Fletcher," Ms. Warren said brightly.

They greeted me with enthusiasm and asked for my passport, which I handed over. That bit of business out of the way, Priscilla led me to another desk, where I gave my credit card to a young man, who issued me a special gold Cunard card to use for all onboard purchases. He returned my credit card, and Priscilla and I stepped around the desk and up a short gangway to the ship, where a receiving line of sharply dressed young men and women awaited us.

"This is Jessica Fletcher," Priscilla said to one of them, a sandy-haired fellow with sharp features, and a British accent. "The *famous* Jessica Fletcher. She's our star lecturer this trip."

"I'm afraid that's—"

"Right this way, Mrs. Fletcher," the young man said. "My name is Sandy."

"Of course it is."

Ms. Warren said, "I'll ring you later, Jessica. In the meantime, you're in good hands with Sandy."

Sandy's laugh was easy and warm. "A pleasure to have you aboard, ma'am."

"Thank you. I understand I'm not the only passenger."

"That's for certain. You're one of eighteen hundred on this crossing."

"That many?"

"Yes, ma'am. Not a cabin to be had. A thousand crew, too."

My cabin, Number 1037, was on the One Deck; the *QE2* has thirteen decks. Sandy opened the door and stepped back to allow me to enter. It was a spacious suite with a secured oblong porthole through which to watch the sea. There was a queen-sized bed, a cocktail table and two pale purple club chairs beneath the porthole, and serviceable purple carpeting. Two huge walk-in closets would accommodate Elizabeth Taylor's wardrobe. A television set offered nineteen channels.

The all-marble tan bathroom featured a large dark brown marble sink, tub with a handheld shower head, a bidet, and a basket overflowing with shampoos, soaps, and body lotions. Definitely more luxurious than my bath at home.

A young man of Asian origin came in and introduced himself as my steward. His name was Walter. "Call me for anything, Mrs. Fletcher, day or night."

"Thank you."

"I'll fetch you some ice."

"When will my luggage be brought to the cabin?" I asked Sandy.

"That could take a while, Mrs. Fletcher. A few hours."

"I'm glad I packed necessities in this shoulder bag," I said.

"Always the smart way to travel," he said.

He showed me where my life preserver was stored on a high shelf in one of the closets. "There'll be a drill in a few minutes," he said. "They'll announce it. You'll put the preserver on and gather in the Mauretania Dining Room. That's one deck up, on the Quarter Deck."

"Oh, yes," I said. "I remember that from my last crossing."

"Not your first time?"

"That was twenty years ago, I'm afraid. I was . . . I was with my husband then."

"Well, Mrs. Fletcher, I'll leave you to freshen up. Welcome aboard."

"Thank you. By the way, have you met any of the other lecturers?"

"No, I haven't."

"The acting troupe? Are they on board?"

"I believe they are. I can check for you."

"No need. I'm sure we'll catch up with each other soon enough."

The announcement of the life jacket drill came fifteen minutes later. I read the instructions for putting on my jacket, managed to do it with minimum fuss, and stepped into the long, narrow hallway where other passengers headed for our assigned gathering spot. We went up the wide staircase to the Quarter Deck and into the Mauretania Dining Room, one of five, not including a spot for hamburgers and hot dogs, plus the nightclubs scattered about the ship.

I sat at a table with other passengers and listened to the instructions on what to do in the unlikely event we had to prepare for an emergency evacuation. As I did, I glanced about the large room. The other passengers were mostly older, although there were some younger couples, even a few young families with small children. The day-care center would be busy.

My eyes stopped at a table two removed from me. No question about it. Marla Tralaine, the motion picture icon of decades ago, sat regally. Posed, is more accurate. She was heavily made up; her famous cascading blond hair was immaculately arranged. Others had recognized her, too, and stared.

I looked in the opposite direction, where television's most famous chef, Carlo Di Giovanni, talked with considerable and characteristic animation to others at his table. His flamboyant TV style while whipping up mouthwatering recipes delighted millions of viewers each day.

After we'd received our instructions, the amplified male voice said, "Thank you, ladies and gentlemen, for your attention. You may now return to your cabins."

I stood, thought for a moment, then decided to approach Ms. Tralaine, who continued to sit with her life jacket on.

"Ms. Tralaine?" I asked.

She looked up and cocked her head.

"I'm Jessica Fletcher—the mystery writer."

She wrinkled her aquiline nose; had an unpleasant odor wafted into the room?

I extended my hand.

She took my fingertips in hers, then quickly let go.

"I understand you'll be giving a lecture, Ms. Tralaine."

"Yes." Her voice was low and sensuous.

"Well, I'll be lecturing, too. And I've written a murder mystery play that an acting troupe will perform."

"I see."

"I've written a small part in it for you. For all the lecturers. I hope you'll—"

One of two young men at the table stood and said, "I'm Peter Kunz, Mrs. Fletcher. Ms. Tralaine's manager." We shook hands.

He turned to the others at the table. "This is Tony Silvestrie, Ms. Tralaine's personal trainer." Silvestrie, a tall, deeply tanned man whose sculptured body perfectly filled out his T-shirt, nodded, but didn't rise.

"And this is Candy Malone, Ms. Tralaine's hairdresser." Ms. Malone got to her feet, smiled, and said, "Really a pleasure, Mrs. Fletcher. I love murder mysteries and have read just about every one of your books."

"I'm delighted to hear it," I said.

Marla Tralaine looked supremely bored. She stood and removed her life jacket. "You'll excuse me, of course, Mrs. Fletcher. How nice to have met you."

Her theatrical delivery of the farewell trailed behind as she and her staff sauntered from the room, heads high, as though crossing a stage.

Well, I thought, I might as well rewrite the play to exclude her from the cast. Not a terribly pleasant woman.

Back in my cabin, I replaced the life jacket on the shelf and resumed unpacking things from my shoulder bag. The phone rang.

"Jessica?"

"Yes."

"Rip Nestor here."

"Hello, Rip. You and your actors are on board?"

"Sure are. I was wondering whether we could get together tonight after dinner. Everybody. Do a run-through."

"That will be fine. I met Ms. Tralaine. I'm sure she won't agree to appear."

"Really? No loss."

"Not a problem," I said. "I'll just take out her few lines. Where shall we meet?"

"The Grand Lounge. On the . . . lemme see . . . yeah, right here on the map. The Grand Lounge on the Upper Deck."

"I know it."

"Nine?"

"Okay."

"I'll have the cast there, and the set pretty much put together. That's where we perform."

"See you then."

One of the nice things about dining aboard the *QE2* in its Queens Grill is that there aren't seatings. You can stroll in anytime during the designated hours. I considered taking a nap before dinner, but Priscilla Warren called just as I was about to stretch out on the bed.

"Not disturbing you, am I?" she asked.

"Not at all. But I was contemplating a nap."

"Can't do that," she said, laughing. "You don't want to miss leaving the pier and going out to sea, watching the Manhattan skyline slide by."

"You're right," I said, having forgotten how inspiring that was from my crossing with Frank twenty years ago.

"Meet you up on the Sun Deck in a half hour?"

"Count on it."

I was glad she'd called. It was awe-inspiring as the gigantic ocean liner was guided from the pier by a tugboat and set on her way, the Statue of Liberty standing tall and proud in the distance.

While on the Sun Deck, the uppermost deck of the ship, also called the Helicopter Deck because of the landing pad marked with a large red cross, Priscilla introduced me to Troy Radcliff, the famed mountain climber. He was an imposing man with a white crew cut, deep tan, and trim body beneath the sweatshirt and chino pants he wore. In his eighties? I only hoped I looked half as good when—and if—I reached that age.

"You'll have plenty of time to get to know each other at dinner," Priscilla said. "All the lecturers will be sitting together. Except for Ms. Tralaine. She has her own table."

I was not surprised.

"Seven?" Ms. Warren asked.

Radcliff and I agreed.

You enter the Queens Grill through what's called the Queens Grill Lounge, a comfortable area of stuffed chairs and tables where cocktails are served, as well as afternoon tea. Large windows afford a delightful view of the Atlantic.

The lecturers had gathered there by the time I arrived.

All except Marla Tralaine, of course. Priscilla Warren had created a large seating area, with a chair reserved for me. "This is Jessica Fletcher," she announced. The others stood and offered their hands. I recognized each of them from their appearances on TV, or from photos in the paper. But there was another person in the group whose face was not familiar to me, a slightly plump older woman with twinkling pale blue eyes.

"This is Mary Alice Ward," said Priscilla.

"Hello," I said, shaking her hand.

"Mrs. Ward won a contest in her hometown of Lumberton, North Carolina."

"What sort of contest?" I asked.

"I solved a murder mystery," she replied in a soft southern accent.

I laughed. "That's wonderful," I said. "Was it a real murder?"

Her laugh was as charming as her accent. "Goodness, no, Mrs. Fletcher. My local bookstore held the contest with Cunard. There was a mystery novel without an ending, and readers were asked to solve it. It wasn't very difficult. I knew who did it by the second chapter."

"Good for you," I said. "Maybe you'll solve the play I've written."

Mrs. Ward chuckled. "I certainly intend to try."

I wasn't in the mood for a cocktail, so we headed in for dinner. The Queens Grill is a handsome room. Fine crystal, silver, and china sparkled in the flattering lighting as waiters in white jackets moved quickly, delivering drinks and food. We were seated at a large round table. One of two waiters introduced himself in what I judged to be a French accent, and handed us menus. We all laughed at how extensive it was.

"Where is the Italian food?" Carlo Di Giovanni asked with a flourish of hands.

The waiter, standing at attention, quickly said in response, "We can make something Italian for you, sir."

Ms. Warren chimed in with, "You'll be given the dinner menu each day at lunch. If there's nothing on it that appeals, you can order something else."

The room's sommelier, a huge key hanging from a leather thong around his neck, delivered the list of wines.

"Who's the expert?" Dan Solon, the judge, asked in a gruff, gravelly voice.

We all looked to Di Giovanni.

But Elaine Ananthous, the gardening expert, said in a tiny, singsong voice, "I'll choose one for us." She was a birdlike woman, probably fifty, with thin, color-less, untamed hair and thick glasses. "Mostly California, I see," she said. After a quick perusal, she chose a Hess Collection fumé blanc and a Grigich Hills cabernet.

"No Italian wine," Di Giovanni said.

"California wine is the best," said Judge Solon.

"Whatever happened to the French?" Troy Radcliff

asked. He was handsomely dressed in a double-breasted blue blazer, white shirt open at the collar, and a red-and-blue ascot. His wide smile, which he flashed often, was rendered whiter in contrast to his tanned, creased face.

A lively debate erupted over the relative merits of various types of wine. I didn't take part because although I enjoy a glass of good wine, red or white, California, Italian, or French, it isn't a topic of particular interest to me. I turned to Mary Ward, who had a bemused expression on her pretty face.

"Do you enjoy wine?" I asked.

"Just on special occasions," she said.

"I'm anxious for your reaction to my play."

"I'm sure it will be just wonderful," she said, "considering all the experience you have writing mysteries."

"But not plays," I said. "I'm meeting with the director and cast after dinner for a run-through. Would you like to join me?"

"I wouldn't want to intrude," she said.

"It wouldn't be an intrusion," I said. "I'm hoping all the lecturers will join me, too. I've written them into the play."

"What fun," she said.

"All except—" I nodded in the direction of Marla Tralaine's table.

"She's still beautiful," was Mary Ward's kind reply.

During dinner—which was wonderful, we were told we could order all the caviar and smoked salmon we wanted, which we took advantage of—I announced that I'd included them in the play as minor characters. I wasn't sure how they'd respond, and was pleasantly surprised that they all enthusiastically agreed.

"Do any of us get killed?" Carlo Di Giovanni asked with a hearty laugh.

No one else laughed. They all looked at me with serious expressions.

"No," I said. "None of you gets killed."

Chapter Six

When we arrived at the stage of the Grand Lounge, Rip Nestor and his cast had already assembled, and were in the midst of a read-through of my script. Nestor called a halt and introduced me to the young actors and actresses. I, in turn, introduced them to Priscilla Warren and Mary Ward.

We stood on the stage and looked out over the vast array of chairs and tables. A few were occupied with curious passengers, but most were empty. Priscilla explained that this was the only night the lounge wouldn't be active. Nightly shows featuring musical entertainment would take the stage from now on. My play would be performed each afternoon from two until three.

Ringing the Grand Lounge, one flight above, was the Grand Promenade, off which the ship's many fancy shops were located. Strollers up there could lean on the railing and look down upon the stage.

Eventually, the other lecturers arrived—including,

to my surprise, Marla Tralaine, who appeared at the rear of the vast room, accompanied by her three-person team of followers.

"Ms. Tralaine," I said, going to her and extending my hand. "I'm so pleased you're here."

"I found your idea intriguing," she said. "Ordinarily, I wouldn't do such a thing. But because it's on this lovely ship—and because my manager thinks I would enjoy it—and because it's you, Mrs. Fletcher, I've decided to take part. May I see my script?"

"Of course." As I went to where a pile of scripts lay on a stool, I couldn't help but smile. I was pleased that Marla Tralaine, as pretentious as she was, had decided to cooperate, no matter what her reasons.

I handed her a script, saying, "It's only a few lines, Ms. Tralaine. Just a walk-on."

Her raised eyebrows said she didn't like being relegated to such a minor role.

I added, "But there's plenty of room for improvisation."

I left her and went to where the other lecturers talked with Rip Nestor. Each held a script and seemed to enjoy what they read, judging from the laughter and banter among them. That made me feel good.

In writing the script, I'd created a play within a play, so to speak. The setting was a television studio from which Judge Dan Solon conducted his talk show. His guests on this particular day were the other lecturers. This created the rationale for them to be together. The rest of the cast, the professional actors and actresses hired by Rip Nestor, played the parts of characters working at the studio, or on Judge Solon's staff. Unsure of whether Marla Tralaine would cooperate, I wrote her in as a special guest, making it easy to delete her appearance if necessary. But judging from her having shown up this evening, it looked as though I wouldn't have to do that.

"Shall we run through this?" Nestor asked.

Everyone agreed.

"Places," he said.

The cast disappeared behind curtains shielding them from onlookers in the audience. Mary Ward, Priscilla Warren, and I took seats at a front table and waited for the first act to begin.

The play would open with Rip Nestor addressing the audience, welcoming them, and creating a sense of the fun that was to come. He would explain that the audience viewing the play was also the audience for the taping of Solon's talk show—an audience within an audience.

The set, consisting only of a desk and a few chairs, was supposed to be the cable TV studio where Solon's talk show was taped. The judge sat behind the desk. Seated to his right were Troy Radcliff, Carlo Di Giovanni, and Elaine Ananthous. The professional actors and actresses took their positions as cameraman, floor director, the show's director, its producer, and other studio staff.

Solon read from the script on the desk. "Good evening, and welcome to the Dan Solon Show."

"Cut!" the director said, as written in my script. "I don't like the camera angle. Change it!"

During the dialogue between the actors and actresses, the director, Millard Wainscott, played by a swarthy, leering young man with a lip that curled on demand, established himself as someone intensely disliked by the others.

Solon introduced his guests for the show—Radcliff, Di Giovanni, and Ananthous, followed by, "We have a special guest this evening. Marla Tralaine, the famed movie actress will be joining us later. She'll be starring in a movie to be produced next month for this cable network."

I'd deliberately limited the lecturers' appearance to the first few minutes of the show, using them to set the scene. Once that was accomplished, they wouldn't appear again until the end of the play, when the murder within it was solved. That's when Marla Tralaine would make her entrance.

After a few lines between Solon and his famous guests, the lights dimmed on cue. When they came up again, the taping of the TV show was over, and the lecturers left the stage. This is when the "real" play began.

The story I'd conceived was straightforward. Conflicts between the actors and actresses began to develop as the first act unfolded. There was jealousy between certain cast members, professional and personal. One thing was clear to the audience as the opening act neared its conclusion. The director, Millard Wainscott, was not popular with his colleagues.

A young actress played his estranged girlfriend, Sheila, who was the script girl for the television production.

There was an older character—I hadn't envisioned him as being *that* old when I wrote him into the script— played by an aging actor who, according to Rip Nestor, had literally pleaded for the job. His role was that of Morris McClusky, Judge Solon's producer. Wainscott treated him with scorn and disdain during Act One, and the older man's anger bubbled to the surface each time he spoke.

And then there was the TV show's floor director, whom I named John Craig. He was played by a handsome young black actor, introduced to me as John Johnson. He, too— the character, that is—harbored an intense dislike for the TV show director, Wainscott, because, it developed as the act progressed, Wainscott had stolen Craig's fiancée from him less than a year ago.

Because I knew how Act One was to end, I leaned forward to see the first of four murders played out by those on stage. The script called for Wainscott to be shot to death just as the scene ended. He was to stand alone on the dark stage, illuminated by a single spotlight, and give what amounted to a soliloquy about his ruthless plans to take over the Dan Solon show and

Teller Broadcasting, no matter how many bodies he had to walk over.

"Here it comes," I said to Mary Ward and Priscilla Warren. "Murder number one."

The sound of the gunshot was loud, causing the few people in the audience to gasp. Wainscott, the character played by the handsome, brooding actor, let out a moan; his hands clutched at his chest. He squeezed open theatrical blood contained in a capsule beneath his white shirt, staining the shirt a vivid crimson. He fell to his knees, let out an even louder protest against pain and imminent death, then pitched forward.

Someone up on the shopping promenade applauded.

The lone spotlight dimmed to blackness.

The first act was over.

Lights on the stage came up again. The actor playing Wainscott got to his feet and wiped himself off. Rip Nestor appeared from backstage and asked everyone to gather around him for comments and suggestions. I stepped up onto the stage and said, "That was great. I loved it."

I looked back to where Priscilla and Mrs. Ward sat, then to where Marla Tralaine and her entourage had taken a table in a darkened corner. They were gone. I wasn't surprised. The script didn't call for her to make an appearance until the final act.

The other lecturers had stayed around, offering their positive comments to the cast.

"Okay," Rip Nestor said, "let's run through Act Two."

It was after eleven when the entire play had been rehearsed. I'd hoped Ms. Tralaine would reappear to say her few lines, but she didn't. No matter. Even if she never showed for the actual performance, it wouldn't hurt things. In a way, I almost hoped she wouldn't take part. Her mere presence was disconcerting.

"A word with you, Mrs. Fletcher?"

The question was asked by an actor who did not appear in the first act. In essence, he would become the star of the play because he played Billy Bravo, the detective called to the TV studio to investigate Wainscott's murder. From Act Two until the end, he took center stage, interrogating the suspects, as well as interacting with the audience.

"Of course."

I'd rejoined Mary Ward and Priscilla Warren at the table. "Please, sit down," I said.

"You were wonderful," Priscilla said to the actor, whose name was Jerry Lackman. "How do you remember all those lines?"

"Mostly improvised," he replied. "Once there's a real audience tomorrow afternoon, most of my work will be to draw them into the play and show them a good time. Your script is great, Mrs. Fletcher. Hope you don't mind how much I deviate from it."

"I don't mind at all," I said. "I watched videos of other mystery plays directed by Mr. Nestor. It was obvious that the key was to make it easy for you to improvise."

"You've obviously played many detective roles before," said Mary Ward, who was dressed in a simple, pretty blue dress with pale yellow flowers on it. Her hair was brown, with just a touch of gray. "You certainly are believable."

"Thanks," Lackman said. "I have a lot of cop friends back in New York. I learn from them."

"Are you from New York?" Mary asked.

"Yeah. Born and bred. Sounds like you're from the South."

Mary laughed softly. "Ah certainly am. Brought up on a farm in Burgaw, North Carolina. It means 'mudhole' in Indian."

We joined her laughter.

"Doesn't sound too appealing," Lackman said.

"A beautiful place," Mary said wistfully.

"So, Mrs. Fletcher, I see you've become friendly with Marla Tralaine," Lackman said.

"I wouldn't say that," I said. "I just met her."

"I saw you talking with her," he said. "I figured you might be close."

"Why?"

"Oh, 'cause you're both big names. You know, famous."

"Thank you for the compliment, Mr. Lackman, but our fame is quite different."

"For which you should be very grateful," Mary Ward said, her voice indicating she wasn't sure whether she was out of place making the comment.

She wasn't. I'd meant it exactly the way she'd interpreted it.

"I'd like to get to know her," Lackman said.

"Then I suggest you approach her," I said. "You're both actors. I'm sure she'd be delighted to spend time with you." I knew that was unlikely, but didn't know what else to offer.

"Will you introduce us?" Lackman asked.

"Yes, if the opportunity presents itself. I'd be happy to."

"Nice meeting everyone," he said, standing. "Mudhole, huh? Funny."

When he was gone, Mary Ward said, "It's far beyond my bedtime, I'm afraid. Will you excuse me?"

"Of course," I said. "We'll catch up tomorrow. What's your cabin number?"

She checked her key. "One-oh-three-nine."

"Next to me," I said. "Sleep tight, Mrs. Ward."

"I will, if you call me Mary."

"Of course. And I'm Jessica or Jess."

"Funny, isn't it?" she said once she'd stood and straightened her dress.

"What's funny?" Priscilla asked.

"That he said he's from New York. Sounds to me like a California accent."

"I . . . hadn't noticed," I said.

"I might be wrong," she said. "Good night."

Chapter Seven

I slept soundly, the huge ocean liner's gentle motion plowing the waters of the Atlantic providing a slow, pleasant rocking sensation in which to wrap myself. Of course, the seas at that stage of the trip were relatively calm. Walter, my steward, had told me the captain expected a smooth crossing. But there are never any weather guarantees on the North Atlantic.

I awoke refreshed and ready for my first full day at sea. My initial lecture was scheduled for that afternoon, immediately following the performance of Act One of my play. I'd prepared notes to help me with my speech before leaving Cabot Cove, and had gone over them many times. I was confident it would go well. I don't believe in writing out a speech, and then reading it, or trying to commit it to memory. I prefer—and most professional speakers agree—to use my notes only as memory joggers. If you know what it is you're speaking about, that's generally all that's necessary.

I considered going to the Queens Grill for breakfast,

but decided I was more in the mood for room service. After calling to order a continental breakfast, I wrapped myself in my robe and read the ship's daily schedule of events that had been slipped beneath my door, a slick publication produced by the *QE2*'s social staff. This morning's issue featured a photograph on the first page of our captain, Captain Sir Archibald Marwick, a handsome gentlemen with beard and mustache, right out of central casting. He would be interviewed in front of an audience in early afternoon by the ship's social directress. There was also a mention on page one of my play.

I turned to the second page and was faced with—me! A large photo dominated the page, along with the notice of my lecture. Other pages in the program heralded talks and demonstrations by Judge Dan Solon, chef Carlo Di Giovanni, and plant expert Elaine Ananthous.

Remarkable, I thought, how busy one could be during the five-day crossing. There were first-run movies, dance lessons, a daily tea dance at four featuring the Tommy Dorsey Orchestra under the direction of Buddy Morrow (my kind of music), aerobics classes, computer lessons, shuffleboard, table game tournaments, classical concerts, gambling lessons in the casino, skeet shooting and a golf driving range, and dozens of other things to do. Of course, one was free to simply find a secluded corner and read a fat book on the way across the Atlantic. Aside from my official responsibilities, that was what I intended to do.

Walter delivered my breakfast with what I would

come to learn was a perpetually sunny disposition. On the tray was a note addressed to me, which I opened and read:

Captain Marwick requests the pleasure of your presence on the bridge at eleven this morning for a personal tour.

How wonderful, I thought. I'd heard the *QE2's* bridge was a marvel of technology and navigational gadgetry.

Energized even more by the invitation, I showered in the luxurious bathroom. It was while I was in the shower that I realized the ship's movements had become more pronounced; I had to hold on to the handrails to keep from being pitched out of the tub.

I left the shower and peered through the porthole. Everything was gray, a cocoon of fog and mist. Walter's sunny forecast was fast proving inaccurate.

I applied my makeup and did my hair, chose a blue-and-green pleated plaid skirt, white blouse, tan cardigan sweater, and sneakers, made sure my point-and-shoot camera was loaded and in my bag, and set out for a morning walk. I remembered from having been on the *QE2* twenty years ago that if you took five turns around the Boat Deck, it equaled one mile. That sounded appealing despite the weather. As I climbed the wide, center staircase, I found myself timing the ship's up-and-down motion, allowing its upward motion to help me ascend, and pausing during the downward dips.

I stepped through a doorway to the Boat Deck. A stiff wind caused me to squint and to raise my hand to my face. The sky was obscured by heavy fog. The wind whipped up the sea and sent salty spray into my eyes. The word "invigorating" came to mind. I debated for a moment canceling my planned walk and retreating to the warmth and dryness inside. But then I spotted Mary Ward, my eighty-year-old new friend and sailing companion.

"Good morning, Mrs. Fletcher," she said brightly. She was dressed in a teal sweatsuit, white windbreaker, and white high-top sneakers.

"Good morning, Mary. I didn't expect to see you out here in this weather."

"Bracing, isn't it?" she said, moving her arms as though warming up to run in a marathon.

"To say the least."

As we started walking together, I realized she was steadier on her feet than I was. I chalked it up to her being shorter, closer to the moving deck. I've always been good at rationalizing things like that.

By the time we'd made one full turn of the Boat Deck, the weather had turned even more foul, the mist threatening to become rain.

"Maybe we'd better go inside," I suggested.

"Oh, one more time around," she said.

I had to laugh as I set off with her again. As we walked,

we talked a little about our individual lives. She was a widow; her deceased husband, an internist, was named Frank, as mine had been. She'd taught high school English, had four grown children, and loved reading murder mysteries and doing crossword puzzles, the harder the better. I really liked this woman. She reminded me of some of Cabot Cove's older citizens, their ages not getting in the way of their busy lives.

Having someone with whom to share the second lap made it go faster, and I found us beginning our third turn around the Boat Deck. A few other hearty passengers had joined us by now, including Marla Tralaine's young manager, Peter Kunz, wearing a shiny yellow jogging suit. Despite the cool, wet weather, he appeared to be perspiring, as though he'd already run a number of laps.

"Good morning," I said.

"Morning," he replied.

"Will Ms. Tralaine be joining you?" I asked.

He shook his head. "Not her thing. She's . . . she's a late sleeper. Lucky to see her by noon."

I wasn't surprised at the answer.

"Care to walk with us?" I asked.

"No. I think I'll go in the other direction." His laugh seemed forced to me. "I'm left-handed," he said. "I just naturally move left to right." He walked away.

Mary and I continued on our third lap, at a faster pace this time. The weather had created what movie directors spend thousands of dollars to achieve, an eerie, ethereal atmosphere in which people and inanimate objects on the deck came and went in wisps of fog—there one moment, distorted and vague, then gone the next, only to reappear.

The outer perimeter of the Boat Deck—of most decks on the *QE2*—is lined with massive white lifeboats covered with orange tarps to keep them from filling with sea- and rainwater. There were twenty of them, I was told, with a capacity of more than two thousand persons. They're lowered by winches in the event the ship has to be evacuated.

We stopped in front of the last one on the starboard side of the ship—the nautical dictionary Cunard had sent me held me in good stead—and caught our breath.

"You know, Mary," I said, "this *is* bracing."

She'd moved from my side and didn't answer.

I looked at her. She'd gotten closer to the lifeboat and leaned forward, as though to better see something.

"What is it?" I asked, joining her.

I didn't need an answer because I saw what she had seen—a woman's bare foot poking up through a small gap in the orange tarp. As shocking as it was, my focus for the first few seconds was on the perfectly applied nail polish on her toes—so incongruous, five small spots of vivid crimson in the monochromatic gray gauze world of the *QE2*'s Boat Deck.

Mary Ward looked at me.

I looked down the length of the deck, but saw no one.

The ship suddenly lurched as it slid down into a deep trough and rode up again on the other side of the aquatic depression, causing us to fall against the lifeboat.

"We'd better inform someone," Mary Ward said in a voice so calm she might have been suggesting we get a cup of coffee.

"Yes," I said. "We had better do that."

Chapter Eight

We went through a doorway and to a phone on an unmanned desk. I picked up the receiver and said to the woman who came on the line, "This is Jessica Fletcher. I'm a lecturer on this cruise . . . crossing. I need to speak to . . . Priscilla Warren."

"Priscilla Warren?"

"Yes. She's my . . . I suppose you can call her my guide."

"Please hold on."

When she came back, she said, "I'll page Ms. Warren."

It seemed an eternity before Priscilla said, "Hello?"

"Priscilla. It's Jessica Fletcher."

"Yes, Mrs. Fletcher? Is something wrong?"

"I'm afraid there is."

I explained the reason for my call.

"You stay right at the phone, Mrs. Fletcher," she said. "I need to contact some other people. We'll be there in a few minutes."

Mary Ward and I waited impatiently. It seemed an

eternity before Priscilla arrived, accompanied by the *QE2*'s security officer, a pink-faced, round gentleman wearing a uniform, who was introduced as Wally Prall. With him was the ship's chief medical officer, Dr. Russell Walker, wearing the obligatory white lab coat, a stethoscope about his neck.

"Where is this body?" Prall asked.

"We'll show you," I said, leading them out onto the Boat Deck and down the starboard side until reaching the lifeboat. I pointed to the foot.

Security Chief Prall stepped up onto a metal box secured to the deck and stretched to enable him to loosen some of the fasteners holding the tarp over the lifeboat. He stripped it back, peered over the gunwale, looked down at Dr. Walker, and said, "Deceased female." His words were carried out to sea by the ever-increasing wind.

They stepped down. Prall asked me, "Have you told anyone about this?"

"No," I replied. "I called Ms. Warren the minute we discovered the body."

"Good," he said. "Follow me."

The minute we were inside, Prall picked up the same phone I'd used and issued orders: "I want the starboard side of the Boat Deck closed off. Get a maintenance crew up here. Make it look like something's being fixed."

Dr. Walker made a call: "We have a deceased passenger on the Boat Deck. Starboard side. Send up a stretcher and two techs. Keep it low-key and quiet."

When Walker hung up, Officer Prall said to him, "Back doors all the way. No passenger contact." He said to me and to Mary, "Please come with me."

"Mr. Prall," I said, "I don't mind coming with you. But perhaps Mrs. Ward would prefer to go to her cabin."

"Oh, no," she quickly said. "I'm happy to come with you, sir."

What she hadn't said was, *I wouldn't miss this for the world.*

We followed the doctor and security chief down the interior port hallway until reaching the G Stairway, one of many stairs linking the thirteen decks. We eventually reached the Two Deck, four decks down from the Boat Deck. Dr. Walker led us into his private consulting room and closed the door. Security Chief Prall excused himself, saying he wanted to get back to coordinate the removal of the body.

"Please have a seat," Dr. Walker said, indicating two chairs.

Once we were seated, he leaned back in his swivel chair, formed a bridge with his fingers, and rested his chin on it. His expression as he scrutinized us was that of someone trying to decided whether we could be trusted. I knew that the death of this woman, whoever she was, posed a problem for not only the doctor, but for everyone else charged with the well-being of eighteen hundred passengers sailing to England on what

MURDER ON THE QE2

was, let's face it, an expensive holiday. Death on board is hardly destined to buoy spirits.

"Mrs. Fletcher," the doctor said, coming forward in his chair and smiling, "I am truly sorry that you and your friend here had the unfortunate experience of discovering the body of a fellow passenger. It must have been traumatic for you."

"We managed," Mary Ward said, returning his smile. This was a formidable southern lady.

"I'm sure you understand our need to keep this under wraps," Dr. Walker said.

"Yes, I can understand that," I said. "But can you? Keep it 'under wraps,' as you put it."

"Oh, yes," he said. "Because we tend to have an older passenger population—not exclusively, but generally tending to be older and more affluent—having someone die during a crossing is not without precedent."

I glanced at Mary Ward before saying, "That doesn't surprise me, Dr. Walker. But this obviously wasn't a . . . how shall I say it? . . . this wasn't a routine death of an older person. That foot does not belong to a senior citizen. Besides, unless there was an older passenger who had the foresight to climb into a lifeboat in anticipation of dying, we have—*you* have a murder on your hands."

"I wouldn't jump to conclusions," he said in a tone I found patronizing. "We've had passengers exhibit some rather bizarre behavior in the past."

"Like climbing into a lifeboat with a member of the opposite sex?" Mary Ward asked.

Dr. Walker's eyes opened wide. "You've heard?" he asked.

"I read a great deal," she said, demurely lowering her eyes.

He cleared his throat and said, "The point is that we musn't rush to judgment as to the cause of this passenger's death. That will be determined by an autopsy."

"Performed here on the ship?" I asked.

"No, of course not. We have a morgue on board. We don't advertise that. But we'll be able to hold the body until we reach Southampton. The family will be notified, and they'll make arrangements for an autopsy and eventual disposition of the body."

"What about family on board?" I asked.

"We still have to identify the victim," he replied. "We'll do all we can to ease their grief and to keep this unfortunate incident from spoiling the rest of the crossing for other passengers."

"May we leave?" I asked.

"Will you cooperate?" he asked.

"In not telling others? Yes. But I assure you, Doctor, this will get around. But not through me."

"Not through me, either," Mary added.

"Well, all I can say is that if we all do our best to keep it quiet, we'll achieve some modicum of success. Thank you both."

"Of course."

As we stood to leave, Security Chief Prall returned to the consulting room. He looked harassed; he was out of breath. He ignored us as he leaned on the desk and said to the doctor, "It's the actress."

"Mr. Teller's wife?" Walker asked. "Lila Sims?"

"No," Prall replied.

"Marla Tralaine?" I asked.

Prall turned to me. "That's right. Marla Tralaine."

"Cause of death?" Dr. Walker asked Prall.

He hesitated, took us all in, then said, "It wasn't natural."

"Oh, my," Mary Ward said.

To which I had nothing to add.

Chapter Nine

Priscilla Warren was waiting for me when Mary Ward and I returned from Dr. Walker's office.

"Will you excuse me?" Mary asked. "This has been a stressful start to the day."

"Of course," I said. "We'll catch up later."

Priscilla followed me into my cabin and shut the door. "I'm sorry this had to happen to you, Jessica."

"Don't worry about me," I said. "I'm just shocked and sad that a famous movie actress had to die under mysterious circumstances on the *QE2*."

"Famous actress?"

"Yes."

"Oh, my God," she said, her eyes open wide, her hand coming to her mouth. "Lila Sims? Sam Teller's wife?"

It was my turn to express surprise. "No," I said. "Not Lila Sims. It was Marla Tralaine. Didn't you know?"

"No. I reported the body, but no one told me who it was. Ms. Tralaine? How did she die?"

"I have no idea. That will be determined by your security and medical people, and the authorities in Southampton. My question is what this does to your schedule of lecturers and the play. I assume there will be a cancellation."

"Oh, no," she said with sudden urgency. "There's no need for other passengers to know what happened. Whenever there's a death on board—it happens now and then—we do everything possible to not let the other passengers learn about it and spoil their holiday."

"But surely, with someone as well known as Marla Tralaine, and with the number of people traveling with her, the word is bound to get out."

"Not if we can help it."

"You thought it might have been Lila Sims, Mr. Teller's wife. I didn't even know they were on the ship."

"They asked that we not broadcast it. They're staying up in one of the penthouses. Next to . . . next to Ms. Tralaine's penthouse. They take all their meals there."

"I see. Well, Priscilla, I suppose all I can do is keep my promise not to talk about this with anyone else."

"What about her?" she asked, nodding in the direction of Mary Ward's adjacent cabin.

"Mrs. Ward? I'm sure she'll keep her word, too."

Priscilla moved to the door. "I'd better check in with the social director. In the meantime, I suggest you get ready for your lecture and the play."

"I've been invited for a personal tour of the bridge," I said. "At eleven."

"Then go through with it, by all means. Obviously, Captain Marwick knows about this. The key, Jessica, is for things to go on as they normally would. That's all we can ask."

She left, and I checked my watch. It was nine—two hours before my tour of the bridge. I could stay in my cabin for the next two hours, but my energy level wouldn't allow that. I needed to get out, resume my walk—not on the Boat Deck, of course—and clear my head.

I stepped into the hallway, where Walter, my steward, was about to deliver fresh ice and towels. "Good morning, Mrs. Fletcher," he said, smiling broadly. "A nasty turn in the weather."

"So I noticed. Unexpected?"

"Yes. But on the North Atlantic you can never—"

Mary Ward's door opened.

"I assumed you'd be resting," I said.

"Rest? How could I? I thought I'd move about a bit, see more of the ship."

"Exactly what I'm off to do."

We were about to head for the shops, located on our deck, when Security Chief Prall approached. "Mrs. Fletcher," he said, "I was hoping to find you."

"Yes?"

"I wonder if you would—" He stopped in midsentence and looked at Mary Ward.

"Remember, Mr. Prall, Mrs. Ward and I discovered the body together. In fact, she was the one who spotted it first. So, please speak freely in front of her."

"Oh, yes. I wondered if you'd come with me to Ms. Tralaine's penthouse."

"Of course I will if you want me to. But why?"

"We found something there that should interest you."

"Then let's go," I said. Before he could protest, I added, "Come on, Mary."

The QE2's thirty-two penthouse suites are accessed via the Queens Grill Lounge. Prall led us through a doorway and up a carpeted staircase with a light wood banister to where a distinguished-looking gentleman in uniform stood at attention.

"This is Mr. Montrose," Prall said, "gentleman's gentleman to our penthouse guests."

The tall, proper Montrose nodded and stepped aside for us to pass.

Prall led us down a hall to the Queen Mary Suite. The door was closed. He knocked. Marla Tralaine's personal trainer, Tony Silvestrie, opened it. He wore gray gym shorts, a white T-shirt that showed off his impressive physique to good advantage, and sandals. He looked at Mary Ward and me as though we'd dropped in from a foreign planet.

"Excuse us," Prall said, sounding official.

Silvestrie frowned, then did as he'd been instructed.

The Queen Mary Suite defined opulence. It was a duplex, one of two "First Suites" out of the thirty-two, the other being the Queen Elizabeth Suite next door. While all penthouses contained a balcony, the First Suites had two of them, one enclosed in glass to allow the occupants to enjoy the outdoors even in inclement weather.

We stepped into the large living room where Silvestrie stood alongside Candy Malone, Marla Tralaine's hairdresser, and two uniformed members of the ship's security staff.

"This is Jessica Fletcher," Prall said. They muttered greetings. "Would you come with me, please? Mrs. Ward can wait here."

I followed Prall into the larger of two bedrooms. He went to a nightstand, picked up a sheaf of paper, and handed it to me. It was a copy of the script I'd written. I glanced at it, looked up at him, then said, "Yes?"

"It's your script, isn't it?"

"I wrote it."

"No," he said. "What I mean is that it seems to be your personal copy, with notes written all over it."

I examined it more closely; there were copious notes on every page. I said, "You're right. There are many notes. But I didn't write them."

"Who did?"

"I believe this is the copy used by the play's director, Mr. Nestor."

"Sure about that?"

"Yes. I saw him use it during the rehearsal last night.

These are his stage directions—ideas about how characters should move and speak, motivation and such."

"Any idea why Ms. Tralaine would have *his* copy in her cabin?"

"No idea at all, Mr. Prall. Maybe he gave it to her to study."

Prall shook his head. "I doubt that," he said. "I talked to her manager, Mr. Kunz. He told me she wanted no part of being in the play, didn't take part in the rehearsal. True?"

"True that she didn't take part. But she told me she would participate."

"When did she tell you that?"

"When she came to the rehearsal."

"But she didn't rehearse."

"No. She left before we finished. But that isn't strange, Mr. Prall. She had what amounted to a walk-on at the very end of the play."

"Any idea where she went after leaving the rehearsal?"

"No."

"Okay. Mrs. Fletcher. Thanks for coming."

"Call on me any time," I said. "By the way, how was she killed?"

"I'm not at liberty to discuss that."

"I understand. I assume I can leave now."

"Of course. And we're still keeping this quiet, Mrs. Fletcher."

"With all those people out there knowing?"

"We're doing our best."

"And I'll cooperate."

Mary and I left the penthouse and stood in the hall. She had a strange expression on her face, a puzzled one.

"Did you notice?" she asked.

"Notice what?"

"The odor in Ms. Tralaine's suite."

"What odor?"

"Garlic. Very pronounced."

"Oh? Probably from something she ordered from room service."

"I didn't see any trays. Did you?"

"No, I didn't."

Mr. Montrose, the gentlemen's gentleman, was busy in a small galley near the top of the stairs. I poked my head in and asked, "Did Ms. Tralaine order room service last night or this morning?"

"No, ma'am. She had dinner in the Queens Grill, as I understand. There was no room service."

"You're right," I said. "I saw her at dinner."

He turned to continue the chore I'd interrupted. As he did, I noticed a roster of passengers occupying the penthouses. Mr. and Mrs. S. Teller were listed in the Queen Elizabeth Suite, next to Marla Tralaine's quarters. Written in red next to their names was SPECIAL MENU.

Mary and I went down the stairs, grasping the banister to keep from falling.

"Still want to go shopping?" I asked.

"I think I will get some rest," she said. "If you don't mind shopping alone."

"Of course I don't. But can I ask you a question?"

"Yes."

"Why are you interested in a garlic smell in Marla Tralaine's penthouse?"

She shrugged and said, "I'm very sensitive to odors, Jessica. We don't use much garlic in southern cooking. I fry most everything. My grits and molded gelatin salads are quite popular in Lumberton." She laughed. "Except my children aren't always crazy about my cooking. But I like Italian food with plenty of garlic when I visit Italy. When I was introduced to that Italian fellow who has the cooking show on television, I smelled a lot of garlic on his uniform."

"Uniform? Oh, his white chef's outfit. Come to think of it, I noticed that, too."

"Just an observation," she said. "Means nothing. Thank you for letting me tag along."

I watched her walk away and couldn't help but shake my head and smile. I felt a little like Sherlock Holmes, Mary Ward my Dr. Watson.

Garlic in the air in Marla Tralaine's penthouse.

Rip Nestor's copy of the script there, too.

This was shaping up to be a memorable crossing.

I detoured on my way to the shops through the Queens Grill where breakfast was being cleared and preparations were under way for lunch. I spotted one of the waiters serving my table, the one with the

French accent. The tag on his uniform said his name was Jacques.

"Good morning, ma'am," he said.

"Good morning."

"You missed breakfast."

"Yes. I had it in my room. I wonder if you would do me a small favor."

"*Oui*. Whatever you ask."

"I've been told that Mr. and Mrs. Teller, in the Queen Elizabeth Suite, have a special menu they enjoy each evening."

He laughed. "*Oui*. They certainly do."

"I'd love to know what it is. I hear it's a very healthy diet. I could use a healthy diet."

"Pasta," he said without hesitating.

"Pasta?"

"*Oui*. For lunch and dinner. Extra-virgin olive oil for Mrs. Teller—Ms. Sims—and red sauce for Mr. Teller. With plenty of garlic. We laugh about it in the kitchen. With all the wonderful dishes available, they eat only pasta and salad. And fruit for dessert."

"It does sound healthy," I said.

"And boring," he said, chuckling.

"That, too," I said. "Thank you."

"Will I see you at lunch?"

"I think so."

"Pasta for you?"

"We'll see. Thanks again."

Chapter Ten

I bought a few inexpensive gifts to bring back to my friends in Cabot Cove, but mostly just browsed the lovely shops along the promenade. At a few minutes before eleven, I met up with an escort who took me up to the bridge high above the ship, where the captain and his officers guided us across the Atlantic.

Captain Marwick was as charming as he was handsome, and the young men and women working under his command that morning looked as though they'd stepped out from a military recruiting poster.

The QE2's bridge, rising almost a hundred feet into the air, is spacious, with windows affording the crew a hundred-and-eighty-degree vista. I assumed the view from there on a clear day was spectacular. The problem was that the weather obscured even the bow of the ship. It was like sailing into oblivion; would we fall off the edge of the Earth any minute? I mentioned this to Captain Marwick.

He laughed and said, "Not a problem, Mrs. Fletcher.

Last I heard, the Earth was round. Then again, I might have had a second-rate public education."

I laughed along with him. "But what if there's another ship out there?" I asked. "Just beyond where we can see?"

That's when I received a lesson in the ship's state-of-the-art navigational equipment—the radar scanning twelve miles in all directions, the technology so advanced that trained radar observers can differentiate a ship from a large wave, an iceberg from a whale. Everything is fed into computers, which plot the *QE2's* course. Aside from needing a human hand when leaving a port and entering another, the passage across the Atlantic is controlled by the autopilot. The crew never touches the controls once the course, speed, and other factors are entered into the system.

"How fast are we going?" I asked.

"Thirty-one knots," he replied. "Quite fast. We're riding the North Atlantic Drift, as it's called. The Gulf Stream, actually."

Before leaving the bridge, I learned that the officers received reports on the ice flow every six hours from spotter aircraft operating from land to our north; that it takes three-quarters of a mile to stop the *QE2*; that the ship has nine large engines, with one always being maintained aboard while the other eight do the work (each consuming two tons of fuel an hour); and that only the captain can order a change in direction or speed, which means he's on-call twenty-four hours a day. He has an onboard apartment, which he shares with his wife, who accompanies him on many crossings.

"This was fascinating," I said. "Thank you for the opportunity to learn about it."

"My pleasure," the captain said. "Let me show you something else."

Off each side of the bridge was an outdoor deck area. Captain Marwick led me out onto one of them.

"Must be lovely in fair weather," I said, pulling my sweater closer.

"Yes, it is. Mrs. Fletcher, I personally wanted to express my regret over the unfortunate incident this morning."

"Ms. Tralaine? Thank you. A tragedy."

"Especially that you had to be the one who discovered her body."

"I appreciate that, Captain Marwick. But anyone could have been the one to spot her in the lifeboat. I just happened to be there, along with a friend."

"You know that we try to keep such incidents quiet for the sake of our other passengers."

"I've been informed of that—many times, by many people."

"I'm sure of that," he said. "But my message to you is that while we would appreciate discretion in this matter, I don't want you to feel burdened. After all, *you* are one of those passengers we're committed to serving. *You* are to have a pleasant and pleasurable crossing, too."

"And I'm sure I will. But thank you for reminding me of it."

My escort held open the door for me, and I followed him down a cramped staircase, wide enough for only one person at a time to pass. When we reached the bottom, another uniformed escort waited to come up. Next to her was a familiar face, the journalist and commentator, James Brady.

"Jim," I said, "I didn't know you were on board."

He smiled, and we shook hands. "But I knew you were, Jess," he said.

"Of course you did. That's your business, knowing who's where." James Brady is probably the country's leading chronicler of the comings and goings of the world's rich and famous, appearing on television, and with a column in *Parade* that reaches millions of readers each Sunday.

"How's your play?" he asked.

"Fine, I think. We rehearsed last night."

"I had breakfast this morning with Judge Solon and Troy Radcliff. They said they're enjoying being in it."

"They seem to be having a good time."

"Solon told me that Marla Tralaine isn't having such a good time."

"I . . ."

"I've been trying to grab an interview with her. Have you seen her today?"

"I . . . yes. I saw her."

"Her manager, Pete Kunz, won't let anyone near

her. I saw her at dinner last night, but I was busy with
Pam Fiori and Mike Cannon from *Town and Country*,
Peggy Cass, and a couple of British writers."

"Good company. Going up to the bridge, Jim?" I
asked with exaggerated animation. "It's a wonderful
experience."

"I've been up there before, but—"

"Great seeing you again. We'll catch up later."

He looked at me quizzically as I quickly walked away.

James Brady aboard?

Other journalists?

*Keep Marla Tralaine's murder a secret for the next
four days?*

Try keeping a British royal scandal quiet.

I freshened up in my cabin in preparation for going to
lunch in the Queens Grill. The rough weather we'd encountered really hadn't bothered me much until now.
But as I again made my way up the main staircase, holding on tight to the banister and practicing going with the
up-and-down flow, I experienced the first twinge of
stomach upset. Nothing major, just a general queasiness
that came and went.

I considered returning to my cabin to put on the
wristbands I'd brought with me, or to apply a seasickness patch. But I decided my upset wasn't serious
enough to make the extra trip.

I entered the lounge and was heading for the dining
room when Elaine Ananthous looked up from where

she sat next to a window. "Mrs. Fletcher," she said, "I was hoping I'd see you before this afternoon."

The chair across the coffee table was unoccupied, and I took it. "Yes?" I said.

She looked left and right, leaned over the table, and said, "I have shocking news."

"You do?"

"Yes." Another glance to ensure she wasn't being overheard. "Marla Tralaine?"

"Yes?"

It was now a barely audible whisper. "She's dead."

I nodded.

"And not by natural causes, Jessica. She's . . . been murdered!"

"I, ah . . . I heard something about it."

"You did?"

"Yes, and the captain wants us to—"

"Where did you hear it?"

I shrugged. "It doesn't matter."

"Do you know how she died?"

"No."

"They found her in a lifeboat."

"Oh?"

"Naked in there."

That was something I didn't know.

"I'm so worried, Jessica."

"Worried about what?"

Her eyes opened wide. "Of being killed like her."

"Why would you think her death would mean that?" I asked.

"There's a murderer loose on this ship," she said. "Marla Tralaine was on this crossing for the same reason you and I are, to lecture. Maybe someone wants to kill all the lecturers before we reach Southampton."

"I seriously doubt that, Elaine. We're not the great chefs of Europe."

"What does that mean?"

"Nothing. Having lunch? I'm starved."

"How can you eat at a time like this?"

"To stop being hungry. Come on. We can discuss this later."

"I couldn't," she said.

"All right," I said, standing. "I'll see you at the play."

Mountain climber Troy Radcliff, Judge Dan Solon, and TV chef Carlo Di Giovanni were already at the table when I arrived. Grim expressions were fixed on the chef's and judge's faces. Did they know about Marla Tralaine, too?

"Hi," I said, allowing Jacques, the waiter, to hold out my chair for me.

"Hello," Radcliff said.

"Looks like I've intruded on a wake," I said.

Di Giovanni said, "This weather. I tried to prepare some of my recipes this morning for my lecture. Everything slides off the table. How can I create with that going on?"

I turned to Dan Solon. "And what has you down in the dumps, Judge?"

"A rejection on my book. I got this fax this morning from my agent in New York." He handed it to me.

"Just one rejection?" I said, handing back the short fax. "I'm sure your agent has submitted it to dozens of good publishers."

"My agent is a jerk. How's your agent?"

"My agent is wonderful."

"What's her name?"

"His name is Matt Miller."

"I just sent a fax to my agent. I fired her."

"Isn't that a little premature?" I asked.

"I don't believe in hanging on to losers. I'll give you my manuscript. You can send it to this Miller guy."

I ignored his brusque demand, preferring to focus upon the assumption that none of them had heard about Marla Tralaine's demise.

Troy Radcliff flashed a smile at me and said, "Unlike our distinguished colleagues, Mrs. Fletcher, I have never been in better spirits."

"How can you be in this weather?" Di Giovanni asked, disgustedly.

"Nothing compared to the weather when scaling Everest," said Radcliff, launching into a lengthy tale of having climbed that famed mountain.

Looking as spry as usual, Mary Ward arrived just as appetizers of caviar, smoked salmon, and shrimp cocktails were delivered. She ordered a simple salad for lunch. Smart lady, I thought. I decided to be prudent for at least one meal and ordered the same.

"Troy was telling us about the time he climbed Mount Everest," I said.

"Times I climbed it," he corrected. "Three times, each one more challenging than the previous attempt."

Conversation pretty much followed the pattern established early in the lunch—complaints from Carlo Di Giovanni and Judge Solon about the weather and literary agents, and tales of mountain climbing from Troy Radcliff. I kept waiting for Elaine Ananthous to change her mind and join us. I was relieved that she didn't, although I couldn't come up with any rational reason for worrying about the news of Marla Tralaine's murder becoming public. It certainly wasn't my responsibility, beyond not personally spreading it.

I glanced often at Mary Ward, who slowly ate her salad and listened to what the others said. What was going through her mind about having found the famous actress's body? If it had upset her, she didn't show it.

"No dessert, thank you," I told Jacques. To the others I said, "Well, everyone ready to take the stage?"

"Is it that time already?" Radcliff asked.

"One-thirty," I said. "The curtain goes up at two."

"There is no curtain," Solon muttered.

"Just a figure of speech," I said. "And I won't ask any of you to break a leg."

"I'll have the raspberries," Di Giovanni told the waiter. "And cappuccino."

"Chocolate mousse cake for me," Solon said.

"The assorted sorbets," said Radcliff. "But no pineapple."

"Why no pineapple?" Judge Solon asked as though Radcliff's request was worthy of a life sentence.

"Because I don't like pineapple," Radcliff said.

Solon grunted and took a cookie from a tray Jacques had set on the table.

"I'm leaving," I said. "See you in the Grand Lounge."

"I'll come with you," said Mary Ward.

After we'd passed through the Queens Lounge, she said, "Would you have time for a brief detour, Jessica?"

"I think so. Where?"

"The Boat Deck."

"Do you really think—?"

"I stopped up there before coming to lunch. Everything is quite normal."

"All right," I said. "Let's go to the scene of the crime."

"Exactly," she said, setting a brisk pace.

The weather was still foul, although the wind seemed to have abated. A few hearty souls walked off their lunch, oblivious to what had occurred earlier that day.

We went to the lifeboat where Mary had first spotted Marla Tralaine's bare foot sticking out. The tarpaulin had been refastened securely to the lifeboat's gunwale.

"How high do you think it is from the deck to the boat?" Mrs. Ward asked.

"I'm bad at judging distances," I said. "Six feet? Eight?"

"About," she said, her eyes narrowed as she came up with her own estimate. "It would take a strong person to lift a body up there, wouldn't it?"

"Yes, it would," I replied. "But of course, that's assuming she was killed elsewhere and brought here. It seems more likely to me she was killed right up there in the boat."

"A distinct possibility," she said. "But if she wasn't killed in the boat, it would mean someone with considerable strength brought her here. A man."

I thought for a moment, then said, "If she was murdered elsewhere, Mary, it could have been a woman who killed her, but who had a male accomplice to help dispose of the body."

"I thought of that, too, Jessica. Well, I just wanted to come up here and run my thoughts by you. I suppose it's time to get to the Grand Lounge."

It was after we'd taken seats at a front table in the crowded lounge, and Rip Nestor was about to come out to welcome the audience, that Mary Ward leaned close to my ear and said, "Mr. Radcliff doesn't like pineapple."

I turned to her. "That's what he said."

"Marla Tralaine didn't like pineapple, either."

"She didn't?"

"No. I read an interview with her years ago. The interviewer asked about her preferences in food, what she liked to cook, things like that." She laughed. "I remember Ms. Tralaine saying that she never cooks. I suppose when you're a big star, other people cook for you. I would never want to be in that situation. I love to cook. Do you?"

"Yes. Sometimes. Marla Tralaine said during the interview that she didn't like pineapple?"

"That's right."

"Interesting," I said, not knowing why.

Rip Nestor, dressed in white slacks and shirt, bounded out to the stage apron and announced, "Good afternoon, ladies and gentlemen, and welcome to an hour of murder and mayhem, mischief and manslaughter."

"She didn't like pineapple?" I said absently.

"No, she didn't." Mary put her index finger to her lips. "Sssssh," she said, smiling. "I want to hear every word."

Chapter Eleven

The first act of the play went well, judging from the audience's active and willing participation. They applauded wildly, booed the character Millard Wainscott, and shouted their approval when he was gunned down at the end of the act.

My fellow lecturers also appeared to have enjoyed playing their small parts at the beginning of the scene. All of them, that is, except the plant lady, Elaine Ananthous. She was a nervous wreck on stage, wringing her hands and allowing an active tic in her left eye to run amuck. I suppose I couldn't blame her. But I was afraid she'd fall apart up there and start screaming that Marla Tralaine had been murdered. Thank goodness she didn't.

Nestor announced to the audience that the second act would be performed tomorrow—same time, same place. He added, "But don't go away. The famous mystery writer, and our playwright, Jessica Fletcher, will be giving her first of two talks right here in just a few minutes."

Mary Ward and I went backstage to congratulate the cast. My antenna was fully extended to pick up on any mention of Marla Tralaine. But only Elaine Ananthous demonstrated unusual behavior. She kept her eyes glued to me, her pinched face set in an expression asking: *What do we do now?*

I managed to catch a few minutes alone with her.

"I thought I'd fall apart out there," she said in her small voice. "I'll never be able to get through my lecture tomorrow."

"Elaine," I said, "I assure you, there is nothing for you, or any of us, to be concerned about. I know how hard it is to carry the knowledge that Ms. Tralaine has been killed, and to have to keep it quiet. But I'm certain that by tonight the word will have gotten out anyway, lifting that burden from us."

"Who could have done such a thing?" she asked.

"I don't know."

Although I hadn't been forthcoming with her when she asked earlier how I'd learned of the actress's death, I didn't let that deter me from asking her the same question.

"I wouldn't want to get the person in any trouble," she replied.

"I won't tell anyone," I said, meaning it.

"It was . . . it was her hairdresser."

"Ms. Tralaine's hairdresser—Ms. Malone, is it?"

"Yes."

"Why did she tell *you*?"

"I don't think she meant to. I saw her standing alone down by the spa. I'm always looking to do something with this thin hair of mine, and I thought she wouldn't be offended if I asked her advice. When I approached, I saw she'd been crying. I asked what was wrong, if I could help. And then she just blurted out that Ms. Tralaine was dead—murdered, found naked in a lifeboat."

"What time was this?" I asked.

"I don't know exactly. Maybe eight. A little after that."

I did a fast calculation. Mary Ward and I had discovered the body at approximately eight o'clock. If Tralaine's hairdresser, Candy Malone, knew about it at eight, that raised serious questions about how she'd learned of it so fast. If it was, as Elaine Ananthous thought it might have been, sometime *after* eight that she approached the hairdresser, that would have given her time to hear about it.

But from whom?

Granted, shipboard scuttlebutt could be an incredibly efficient and rapid conveyer of information. But not *that* fast. From what I'd observed, the attempts to put a lid on the murder had been successful, at least at that early hour.

I changed the subject.

"Tell me what you'll be lecturing about," I said.

"Poison," she replied.

"Poison?"

"I know it sounds silly, but since so much of what's going on during the crossing has to do with murder—your lectures and the play, I thought I'd discuss poisonous plants and how they've been used in murder mysteries to . . . kill people."

She was about to break into tears.

"That sounds like a wonderful lecture," I said, forcing enthusiasm into my voice.

"Maybe I shouldn't do it," she said. "I could say I'm sick."

"But then you'd miss the fun of the crossing. No, you give your lecture on poisonous plants. I'm sure it will be fascinating."

I hadn't noticed that Mary Ward had joined us. When I did, I told her the subject of Elaine Ananthous's lecture.

"I always enjoy mysteries where poison is the instrument of death," she said. "I don't like blood and gore, guns and knives. Give me a good old-fashioned poisoning any day."

I smiled and said, "I tend to agree with you."

" 'How oft hereafter rising shall she look; through this same garden after me—in vain.' "

She answered our quizzical expressions with, "It's from the *Rubaiyat*. A favorite of mine. I love poetry."

"We'd better break this up," Rip Nestor cut in suddenly. "You've got a full house waiting for you, Jessica."

"Thank you," I said. "I almost forgot I'm supposed to speak."

Priscilla Warren, whom I hadn't seen since the dismaying events of earlier that day, suddenly appeared. "Sorry I'm late," she said. "I'll introduce you."

Working from a biography supplied by my publisher, she breathlessly rolled through a list of my publishing credits. The audience applauded as I stepped from the wings and approached the microphone. But Priscilla intercepted me halfway there and whispered, "The word is getting around about Ms. Tralaine. If anyone asks about it, please say you know nothing."

I spoke for almost forty-five minutes, tracing the history of the murder mystery, mentioning the basic types, and talking about how I'd been influenced by great mystery writers, past and present. I then asked if there were any questions.

There were, many of them. But no one mentioned Marla Tralaine.

The other lecturers, who'd stayed after the play to hear me, were congratulatory, as were Priscilla Warren and Mary Ward.

I looked at my watch. "I did go on, didn't I?" I said, shaking my head. "It's four. The tea dance is starting."

"A word, Mrs. Fletcher?"

Jerry Lackman, the actor who would make his appearance as Detective-Sergeant Billy Bravo in tomorrow's second act as the officer called to the TV studio to investigate Millard Wainscott's murder, beckoned me to join him apart from the group.

"Yes?" I said after we'd moved a few feet away. "Oh. You wanted me to arrange an introduction for you with Marla Tralaine. I'm afraid it's too—"

"Yeah, too late," he said. "She's dead."

"You know."

"I know."

"The captain has asked us to not publicly discuss it," I said.

"I know that, too. What did they tell you, Mrs. Fletcher?"

"Very little."

"You discovered her body."

"Yes, I—actually, Mrs. Ward over there made the discovery. I was with her. How did you learn about it?"

"The word's getting around."

"That I discovered the body?"

He nodded.

"No one in the audience seems to know."

"They're keeping it in official channels."

"Why would that include you, Mr. Lackman?"

"Call me Jerry. I didn't mean I was official or anything. I guess I get too wrapped up playing a detective. Live the part."

Somehow, I didn't believe him.

"Jessica," Troy Radcliff said. "You promised me the first dance."

"I did?"

I watched Lackman go to where other cast members congregated, and replayed our brief conversation over in my mind. *Official channels?* I'd make it a point of asking him about that the next time we spoke.

The daily four o'clock tea dance featuring the Tommy Dorsey Orchestra was held in the Queens Room on the Quarter Deck, one level below. As we walked there, the music acted as a magnet, drawing us down a wide, carpeted hallway with large windows looking out over the sea, and to the sprawling nightclub's dance floor, surrounded by comfortable chairs and tables. Waiters and waitresses in white jackets sliced through the dancers already on the floor, carrying tea services, finger sandwiches, and sweets on large trays. It was filling up fast; we were fortunate to take the last empty cluster of chairs, six in all, just to the right of the band.

The beat was infectious. Despite the motion of the ship as it plowed through the rising swells of the North Atlantic, the dancers seemed to be doing just fine. The band, led by the veteran trombonist Buddy Morrow, whose *Night Train* was a huge success decades ago, consisted of fifteen young musicians playing the familiar arrangements of the original Dorsey band. I noticed that everyone at our table—everyone in the large room—was tapping their feet along with the music. A male singer stepped to the microphone and joined the band in one of its biggest hits, "I'll Never Smile Again," a favorite of mine. Although the vocal group that appeared on the recording, the Pied Pipers, wasn't there, I could hear them harmonizing with the singer.

"Jessica?"

Troy Radcliff had stood and offered me his hand.

"I haven't danced in so long," I said.

"You never forget," he countered.

He led me to the floor, and we settled into a pleasant, moderate dance step.

"See?" he said. "You haven't forgotten."

My thoughts were on my late husband, Frank. He was never comfortable on a dance floor, but was a trouper whenever I was in the mood. I always missed him. But it was at times like this that the ache was more acute.

The band picked up the tempo with another all-time favorite, "Marie."

"A little too fast for me," I said.

As we returned to our table, Mary Ward was heading for the dance floor on the arm of one of the *QE2*'s eight "gentlemen hosts," older men whose duty during a crossing is to provide dancing partners, as well as conversationalists, for the single women.

Mary's partner was a handsome chap, tall and slender, with a ruddy complexion and looking very nautical in his white slacks and shoes, and blue open-neck shirt. His hair was yellow-white, which he slicked straight back. I broke out in a smile as Mary followed his expert lead, a grin on her face.

My focus was, of course, on her. But as I watched

them navigate the dance floor, I found myself looking more intently at her partner. I had the nagging feeling I'd seen him before. Could he have been aboard twenty years ago when Frank and I made the crossing? I doubted it. He would have been too young then to be hired for such a job.

It had to have been in another setting. Maybe during my travels to promote my books. He looked British to me, although that was a stereotypical guess on my part.

He delivered Mary to the table, thanked her for the dance—in a British accent—and asked if I would like to join him on the floor. The band was playing "Song of India," its tempo still a little fast for me. But my curiosity got the better of me.

"It's a pleasure dancing with the famous Jessica Fletcher," he said as we fell into step.

"You may not say that when you're finished dancing with me," I said.

"Oh, no," he said, guiding me into a turn. "You're very smooth. Very smooth, indeed."

"I was watching you before," I said. "You look familiar."

"Can't imagine why," he said. "Enjoying the crossing?"

Had I been totally honest, I would have admitted that finding the body of a famous movie actress had tempered any enjoyment I might be feeling. But I said,

"I'm having a marvelous time. Are you with the ship everywhere it goes?"

"I've just recently signed on, Mrs. Fletcher, but I will be staying with it for the year. We do a round-the-world cruise later on. I'm looking forward to that."

His voice mirrored his cultured appearance—deep and resonant. A trained voice, I thought.

After returning me to my group, he went on to dance with other unattached women. The more I looked at him, the stronger became the feeling that his face was familiar.

The dance ended at five. I've always felt that afternoon tea, a British tradition, was one of the world's more civilized pleasures, and this afternoon hadn't changed my opinion. Of course, most teas aren't accompanied by such splendid swing era music. By the time it was over, I'd actually forgotten about Marla Tralaine, at least for the moment.

I'd just walked into my cabin when the phone rang. It was the ship's director of security, Wally Prall.

"Ah, Mrs. Fletcher, I was hoping I'd catch you."

"You barely did," I said. "Is there something new about Ms. Tralaine?"

"I'm afraid there is. That's the reason for my call. I was wondering whether you'd be good enough to come to a meeting in my office."

"Of course. When?"

"Now?"

"Now? I was going to nap before dinner. How long do you think the meeting will last?"

"No more than a half hour."

"I'm leaving right away."

Present in Mr. Prall's office were Priscilla Warren, the *QE2*'s staff captain, the cruise director, the social director, and a young woman responsible for putting out the daily program that's slipped beneath each cabin door in the early hours. After I was introduced to them, Mr. Prall got to the point.

"Mrs. Fletcher, sad to say that word of Ms. Tralaine's tragic death is beginning to make the rounds."

"I'm not surprised," I said.

The cruise director said, "I've been in telephone contact with our public relations people in New York and London. It's their feeling that we should come out with one statement, with a single spokesperson, to put to rest any wild speculation."

"Well," I said, "I'm not a public relations expert, but that makes sense to me. If everyone finds out through gossip and word of mouth, they'll naturally begin conjuring all sorts of theories and become unnecessarily frightened."

"Exactly," said the social director.

"Precisely," said the staff captain.

I felt all eyes on me.

"Is that what you wanted me here for?" I asked. "To agree with your approach?"

"No," said Prall. "We were hoping you would agree

to be the spokeswoman for us. Write a story about it for tomorrow's program. And be available each day at a specified time to answer passenger questions and give a daily update."

"Me? Why me?"

The social director said, "You have considerable stature, Mrs. Fletcher, to say nothing of credibility with millions of readers, many of whom are on this crossing. Naturally, Captain Marwick would be the logical choice. But it's felt he'd best stay aloof from it and tend to those duties passengers expect him to be performing, namely guiding us safely across the North Atlantic. He quite agrees with that."

I started to say something, but the cruise director said, "We realize it would cut into your free time, but we're asking only for perhaps an hour a day. And for your considerable writing talents to be utilized tonight for tomorrow's program."

"I—"

"We've run this by our public relations people," said the staff captain. "They applaud the idea. In fact, they're so appreciative that they've authorized me to award you another crossing in the future, for you and up to three friends, at absolutely no cost to you or to them."

"That's very generous, but—"

"Please say yes, Jessica," Priscilla Warren said. "It would mean so much to the other passengers to hear your calming voice."

"Go over again what it is you want me to do," I said.

When Prall had, I said, "All right. But on one condition."

"Anything, Mrs. Fletcher," the social director said.

"That I be kept fully informed of everything having to do with Ms. Tralaine's murder."

"We were hoping not to use that term," Prall said.

"But she was *murdered*," I said. "If I'm to be the spokeswoman, I insist upon being entirely truthful. I believe that represents good public relations."

"Of course," the staff captain said.

The woman responsible for the program said, "Could we start right now?"

"Write the piece for the program? Yes."

"We'll send dinner to wherever you're working," the social director said.

"That won't be necessary," I said. "I'm sure it won't take very long to write—the truth."

Chapter Twelve

The editor of the shipboard newsletter/program, Rose Jenkins, led me to her office. I suppose the term "office" could be applied to it, although "closet" came more to mind. The closets in my cabin were significantly larger than her working space.

"It's cramped, I know," she said.

"A proverbial understatement. Tell you what, Ms. Jenkins. If you'll tell me how many words you want this to be, I'll just go back to my cabin and write it there."

"Do you have a laptop computer with you?" she asked.

"No. The last thing I intended to do on this crossing was to write."

"I can arrange for the Computer Learning Center to send one up to you."

"I'm not terribly computer literate," I said. "It would have to be a simple word processing program."

"They have them all, Mrs. Fletcher."

After a few minutes of discussion about the piece I was to write, I returned to my cabin to await delivery of a computer. Fifteen minutes later, a young man arrived, carrying a small, portable model. How so much technology could be crammed into such a tiny machine boggled my mind.

"It has three or four of the most popular word processing programs loaded." He named them. One was Microsoft Word, the same program I used back home. Convenient, I thought. I wouldn't have to stumble through something new and unfamiliar.

"You can just deliver this disk when you're through to Rose Jenkins," he told me. "She'll print right from it."

I sat down at the marvelous little machine the moment he was gone. I'd made a few notes of my conversation with Rose Jenkins and quickly perused them. The announcement of Marla Tralaine's death was to be short and to the point. It had been decided during the meeting with Security Chief Prall that rather than meddle with the program's basic format, what I wrote would be included as an insert, no more than five hundred words.

Up until that moment, I had the announcement already written in my mind. It would be a straightforward, classic journalistic approach. Simply tell the reader the who, what, why, where, and when of the incident. I hadn't written anything journalistic for years, but I did remember from my undergraduate days how to construct a story's lead, using what's called the "inverted pyramid."

But the moment I was alone with my thoughts, and the glare of the blank screen, I, too, went blank. It wasn't writer's block as I sometimes experienced when writing my novels. I was unable to focus in this instance because I couldn't shake the face of the gentleman host who'd danced with Mary Ward, then with me.

I got up from my chair, looked through the sealed porthole to the sea, then closed my eyes. When I opened them, the porthole had become, for a fleeting instant, a television screen.

And there he was.

I sat on the bed, went through the shipboard phone directory, picked up the phone, and dialed the number for the library and bookstore. "This is Jessica Fletcher in Cabin ten thirty-seven."

"Yes, Mrs. Fletcher?"

"Since the actress Marla Tralaine is aboard as a lecturer, I was wondering whether you'd brought along videos of some of her movies for this crossing."

"As a matter of fact, we have. Three of them, I think."

"There was a film she did that took place in London, if memory serves me."

"Hold on."

She came back on and said, "I'm reading the backs of the boxes the videos come in. Here it is. It's called *Dangerous Woman*. Her picture is on the box. Very sensuous."

"Yes, that's the one I was thinking of. *Dangerous Woman*. I need to . . . I'd like to see it on my VCR."

"I'll have it sent right up, Mrs. Fletcher. And welcome aboard. We have all your books here. The cruise director said you'd be willing to hold an autographing session some afternoon."

"Of course. I'll get the video back to you right away."

I again tried to start the story of Marla Tralaine's murder, but had only written the first sentence—four times—when Walter, my steward, arrived with the video. He handed it to me, turned to leave, then said, "The captain says it will be getting rougher, Mrs. Fletcher. Sudden storm bearing down on us."

"That isn't good news," I said.

"But not to worry," he said. "This is a fine ship. The best. Built for rough weather."

I nodded. I knew that not only were we on a crossing, not a cruise, despite that there was a cruise director aboard, but also we were on an ocean liner, not a cruise ship, built to much more stringent and demanding standards.

"Thanks for the video, Walter."

"Yes, ma'am. Careful in the shower. Hold on tight."

"I certainly will."

I'd been so engrossed in other things that I'd ignored my mild nausea of a few hours ago and the ship's increased movement. But now that Walter had reminded me, I became well aware of it.

I took the videotape from its box, slid it into the VCR

attached to the TV, pushed the right buttons, and began watching *Dangerous Woman*. I'd seen it before, of course, on cable television prior to leaving Cabot Cove. I tried to run the film at fast-forward, but hit the REWIND button instead. Eventually, I figured out which button did what, and ran the film to where the reason for my wanting to watch it appeared. I leaned closer to the TV screen and narrowed my eyes.

The character played by Marla Tralaine had just entered her lavish London flat. It was raining hard; she was soaked as she stepped inside. The lighting was typical of British filmmakers, low-key and atmospheric, lightning punctuating the eerie interior of the house.

Ms. Tralaine, playing the role of the film's title, discarded her wet outer garments and went to a library where a fire blazed in an oversized fireplace, coats-of-arms and huge oil portraits above it.

A door at the other end of the room opened and a man dressed as a servant entered.

Tralaine snapped at him: "Bring me a brandy, for God's sake! And hurry up."

The camera zoomed in tight on his face. It was twisted as he fought to control hatred of his mistress.

I sat back and conjured up the image of the gentleman host who'd danced with Mary Ward, then with me.

He and the actor in the movie were one and the same.

I played the scene over three more times before rewinding the tape and slipping it back in the box.

What did it mean?

This particular gentleman host, as he's called, mentioned during our dance that he'd recently signed on the *QE2*. Had he done it because he knew Marla Tralaine would be on this specific crossing? If so, what was his motive for doing so?

To rekindle an old flame?

Or to avenge an old hurt?

The phone rang. It was Rose Jenkins, asking how the insert was going.

"Just fine," I lied. "Almost done."

"Just call me when it's finished," she said. "I'll come by your cabin and pick up the disk."

"Give me another hour," I said, "to polish it."

Having resolved my nagging feeling that I knew the gentleman host, my mind was free to get to serious work on the announcement of Marla Tralaine's death. Once I started, my fingers flew over the laptop's keys. I used the built-in spell-checking software, made a few word changes of my own, then called Ms. Jenkins. She was at the cabin in minutes.

"Great," she said after reading on the screen what I'd written.

"I think it accomplishes what the ship's staff wants to accomplish, without unduly scaring anyone."

"I'll get this printed right away," she said. "Have you had dinner?"

"No." I checked my watch. "I still have time to get

to the Queens Grill. Or there's always a hot dog down by the pool."

"Well, thanks so much for doing this," she said. "I think it will go a long way to keeping everyone calm. The word is really getting around now. Other passengers are asking questions."

"Inevitable."

I retouched my makeup, left the cabin, and headed for the Queens Grill. The weather hadn't seemed to dampen anyone's spirits, judging from the laughter as people navigated the stairs, leaning left and right against the ship's movements, or pausing to allow it to rise out of a trough. I remembered from my previous crossing with Frank that those prone to seasickness often ended up in the ship's infirmary, receiving a shot to help them get through the rest of the trip. But these passengers I saw evidently had sound sea legs. Mine were supporting me pretty nicely, too. My minor bout of nausea had passed without the use of wristbands or patches. Despite Walter's warning that a serious storm was bearing down on us, I really didn't anticipate the crossing becoming any rougher.

As I entered the restaurant and was greeted by the handsome, suave maitre d', I wondered whether I'd be dining alone, considering the late hour. I was mistaken. Troy Radcliff, Carlo Di Giovanni, and Mary Ward had just been served their entrees.

"Glad to see you," Radcliff said as Jacques held out my chair. "We were worried about you."

"I'm fine," I said. "I had something to do."

"Concerning Ms. Tralaine's murder?" Di Giovanni asked.

"Yes," I said.

"What kind of cruise is this?" he said with a flourish.

"It's a crossing," I said.

"Crossing, cruise, whatever. The ship bounces us around like a cork in the water, and somebody goes around killing people." He let out a string of words in Italian, unflattering ones I was sure.

"They say it was you who discovered the body," said Radcliff.

"No," I said. "Mrs. Ward saw it first. But we were together, taking a walk on the Boat Deck."

"What were you doing just now that involves her murder?" Radcliff asked.

"Writing an announcement about her death. It will be in tomorrow's program as an insert."

"You write about it?" Di Giovanni said loudly. More Italian came from him.

"It's better to have all the passengers learn about it from one source," I said, giving out the official party line. "It heads off unsettling speculation."

I sensed others in the dining room looking in our direction. I smiled at a few of them, then redirected my attention to my tablemates. "I'd better order," I said.

"How was she killed?" Radcliff asked.

"I don't know," I answered.

"Poison," Di Giovanni muttered.

We all looked at him.

"Poisoned?" Mary Ward said, eyes wide.

"That's what I hear," the TV chef replied.

"Where did you hear it?" I asked.

He shrugged. "The judge."

"Judge Solon?"

"Right." He started to eat his entree, a veal dish he'd specially ordered at lunch.

The ship made a sudden, energetic motion that caused us to lean to the side and grab hold of the arms on our chairs.

Once we were righted again, I took a fast look at the menu and ordered a filet mignon with black pepper and raisin sauce.

Radcliff and Di Giovanni excused themselves once they'd finished their meals, leaving Mary Ward and me at the table.

"Do you think it really was poison that killed Ms. Tralaine?" she asked as Jacques delivered my steak. I don't eat a lot of red meat. But when I do, I like a quality steak. This one certainly was, as good as I've ever tasted in my favorite steakhouse restaurants.

"Sounds like idle speculation to me," I said.

"The sort of speculation you hope to avoid with what you've written about it."

"That's right."

Recognizing the actor from *Dangerous Woman*, now one of eight gentleman hosts on the *QE2*, posed a dilemma for me.

On the one hand, I felt an obligation to share that knowledge with the ship's security staff. On the other hand, his having been in a film with the actress many years ago did not, in itself, indicate he was guilty of any wrongdoing.

There was also the internal debate over whether to tell Mary Ward of my discovery. Because we'd been together when Marla Tralaine's body was found, I considered her a partner of sorts. Besides, she was obviously someone with a keen interest in such things, who'd want to be kept abreast of developments.

I decided to put that decision on hold for a while. There was simply too much happening, at too rapid a pace, to add it to the mix.

"Jessica," Mary Ward said as Jacques cleared my plate and took my order for coffee.

"Yes?"

"If it *was* poison that killed Ms. Tralaine, why would she have been taken to the lifeboat without any clothes on?"

"A good question," I said.

"Unless she was naked when she ingested the poison."

"That's a possibility, too, Mary."

"Ms. Ananthous is going to lecture tomorrow on poisonous plants and their use in murder mysteries."

"That's right," I said. I looked at her. "You aren't suggesting that—?"

"Oh, no. Of course not. It just crossed my mind, that's all."

We left the Queens Grill together, and paused in the lounge to observe the dark sea through the large windows. Although we couldn't observe much, it was obvious this was not a night to venture out onto any deck.

"Jessica!"

James Brady, my journalist friend, entered the lounge. "Buy you a drink?" he asked.

"Thanks, no. This is Mary Ward."

"A pleasure," Brady said. "Jess, can I corner you alone for a few minutes?"

I looked to Mary, who said, "You go right ahead. I read your column in *Parade* every Sunday, Mr. Brady. I like it very much."

"Thank you, Ms. Ward."

"I'm going to the casino," she announced.

"You gamble?" I asked.

"Oh, a little. Some of my friends back in Lumberton gave me money—just small amounts—to gamble for them whenever I'm going to a place that has a casino. A few quarters for the slot machines, that sort of thing. If I win with their money, we share it."

"What a nice idea," I said. "Maybe I'll join you there later."

"Is she a mystery writer, too?" Brady asked as Mary walked away.

"No," I said. "But she could be. Now, you said you wanted to talk with me. About Marla Tralaine, I assume."

"Good assumption. You've known about it from the beginning."

"Yes."

"This morning, when I asked if you'd seen her."

"Again, yes. I didn't feel it was my place to tell anyone about it, especially a member of the press."

"I understand. What *do* you know?"

"Very little."

"I hear you're writing something for the daily program about it."

I forced a laugh. "It isn't as though I'm doing an article, Jim. The Cunard people felt it would be good if all the passengers learned about the tragedy at once, from a single source."

"And you're that source."

"Yes."

"I heard she was stabbed."

"Stabbed? With a knife?"

"No. With some sort of ice pick, like the ones used by mountain climbers."

"Oh?"

"Is that what you've heard?"

"Not exactly."

"Have you been in touch with Sam Teller?"

"The cable TV Sam Teller? No. He and his wife are in seclusion, I'm told."

"Bad blood, Jessica, between Sam Teller and Marla Tralaine."

"I didn't know that."

Brady, as handsome an Irishman as I've ever known and with a charm to match, said, "My TV producer back in New York asked me before I left to file reports from the ship. I told him I didn't want to, unless there was some breaking news. Well, this qualifies."

"I would say so."

"Since you seem to be in the thick of things, Jess, I'd appreciate being kept in the loop."

"For you, James Brady? Of course. Quid pro quo."

"I wouldn't have it any other way."

"Then you keep me in *your* loop, which is always considerable. Deal?"

"Deal. Where are you headed?"

"I hadn't given it much thought. Maybe I'll join Mrs. Ward in the casino."

He reached in his pocket, pulled out two quarters, and handed them to me. "For a slot machine. We'll split the winnings."

Chapter Thirteen

I intended to go straightaway to the casino to meet up with Mary Ward, but on my way there, I took a detour and stopped in at the office of the *QE2*'s director of security, Wallace Prall. I caught him as he was leaving.

"I finished writing the insert and gave it to Ms. Jenkins," I said.

"Good. That's great, Mrs. Fletcher. Very much appreciate it."

"But there's something I think we should talk about."

He looked as though he were in a hurry, so I quickly said, "Theories seem to be running rampant about how Ms. Tralaine was killed."

His face reflected surprise.

I continued, "Some people are saying she was poisoned. And I just heard from someone else that she was stabbed to death with some sort of ice pick."

"That's bound to happen in such a situation," he said.

"I can understand that, Mr. Prall, but don't you

think we should include something in the program about *how* she died? To head off these rumors?"

"You already said you've written the announcement. Too late to change it, isn't it?"

"Probably. But I was thinking more in terms of announcing it in some other way. You suggested I hold a briefing each day on the situation. If I knew how she died, I could mention it tomorrow morning."

"That's good of you to suggest, Mrs. Fletcher, but I think I was premature in suggesting daily briefings. We won't need anything further from you. The insert you've written more than suffices."

His attitude bothered me. I asked directly, "How *was* Ms. Tralaine murdered?"

"I really have to run," he said.

I repeated my question, with more emphasis this time.

"I'm not at liberty to divulge that information."

"Has cause of death been determined?" I asked.

"I'm really sorry, Mrs. Fletcher, but I do have to run. I'm late for a meeting. Her death has us all hopping."

As I watched him walk away, I tried to understand his point of view. Obviously, he had a serious and difficult job to do. Having me—who after all was only a mystery writer and passenger—probing into his area of expertise was undoubtedly annoying.

But they'd reached out to me, and I'd responded. Surely, they owed me at least the courtesy of basic information.

The casino was a beehive of activity when I entered the QE2's large space devoted to gambling. The air was filled with a discordant symphony of bells and whistles from the dozens of slot machines. The roulette tables were three deep, and the two craps tables were doing a land-office business.

I looked for Mary Ward among the slot machine players, but didn't see her, so I wandered over to one of the craps tables where Judge Dan Solon yelled words of encouragement to other players in his deep, gruff voice.

I'm not a gambler, but a friend once took me to a London casino and gave me a primer on shooting craps, saying he enjoyed that game the most because it involved participation with others. Everyone at the table was playing against the house, he explained, with the exception of the occasional person betting the wrong way, placing bets along with the casino, and hoping the other players at the table would lose. These are not especially popular players, according to my friend.

The dice had just been passed to Judge Solon. He blew on them as craps players are wont to do, implored the dice in his hand to be good to him, and energetically tossed them to the opposite end of the table, where they ricocheted off the ridged rubber surface, spinning and tumbling on the green felt, then coming to rest. There was an eruption of excitement; I assumed the judge and his fellow gamblers had won on that toss.

I was going to drift away to renew my search for Mary Ward when I noticed a player at the other end of the table, the older actor who played Morris McClusky in my play. And, to my surprise, wedged in between him and a corpulent male passenger, his round face flushed with the excitement of the game, was my new-found friend from North Carolina, Mary Alice Ward.

Shooting craps? When would she stop surprising me?

She saw me, broke into a grin, and waved for me to join her. It wasn't easy navigating the knot of players at the table, but I eventually made it to her side.

"Mr. Ryan here is teaching me how to play dice," she said.

"Oh," was all I could come up with.

"Craps," he corrected.

Ryan, whose first name was Ron, was a wonderful-looking, stooped older man, with a craggy face that reminded me a little of the actor Walter Matthau. He hadn't fallen victim to male pattern baldness, but his hair had turned a uniform white. He glanced at me and said, "She's my good luck charm for the evening," referring to Mary.

"I hope she brings you good fortune," I said.

The stickman, the casino employee at the table responsible for moving the dice to the proper player, used his long stick to push them back to Judge Solon. I looked down at the table in front of Ryan. He'd placed dozens of chips on a narrow band marked PASS. I didn't know how much the chips were worth, but I assumed they represented quite a bit of money. I checked the piles of chips in front of other players. Mr. Ryan's bet was at least triple anyone else's wager.

Solon again rolled the dice. When they came to rest, one read three, the other four. Again, an enthusiastic response from those at the table. Of course, I thought. Three plus four equals seven, which my friend had told me was always a winner unless . . . unless it occurred at another point in the game; I couldn't remember what that rule was.

Mary said to me, "This is so exciting. I've never seen this game before."

"Did you win any money for your friends, playing the slot machine?" I asked, having to speak loud over the noise from the vocal players at the table.

"Oh, yes. I put in three quarters in a machine over there," she said, pointing, "and got one hundred back."

"That's wonderful," I said, tempted to add that she should take her winnings and leave the casino.

The judge rolled a nine. That seemed to change everything. The casino employees shifted chips to various marked areas of the table. On the next roll the dice came up with a six and a one. There were loud moans as the employees scooped up chips from virtually everyone and put them in the casino's coffers. Now, I remembered. A seven was always a winner unless a different number had been rolled. Then, seven became a loser.

"I'm so sorry, Mr. Ryan," Mary Ward said, her voice heavy with dejection.

"No problem," he said, placing a new supply of

chips on the PASS line. "I have a feeling my luck is going to run good tonight."

I had to smile at his comment. It's what every gambler I've ever known says when they're losing. I had the distinct feeling that Ryan perhaps had a gambling problem. That might have been an unfair judgment on my part, based only upon watching him for a few minutes at a gaming table. But you pick up a sense of those things if you've been around enough people, and are in the business of observing human behavior in order to create believable characters in books.

Rip Nestor had told me Ron Ryan virtually begged him to play the role of Morris McClusky on this crossing. The character I'd created wasn't a major one, although he did play a pivotal role toward the end of the play. I didn't imagine Nestor paid his actors and actresses very much, depending upon the lure of a luxurious five-day North Atlantic crossing to England as a compensation for a lack of hard cash.

Why would this actor beg to be in this play? Obviously, because he was like most actors, always looking for the next job.

Although I wasn't a participant in the game, I found myself mesmerized by it, and stayed there as the dice passed from hand to hand each time someone threw a seven after another number had been rolled.

The stickman, not realizing I wasn't a player, pushed the dice to me. I shook my head. He moved them on to Mary, who looked to me, and then to Ryan.

"Go ahead, toss 'em," Ryan said. "For me."

Mary took a deep breath, picked up the two dice as though they were hot, looked at them in her hand, and asked, "Now?"

"Now!" Ryan said.

She reached as far as she could over the table and tentatively threw the dice to the opposite end. They came up eleven, a winner; along with a seven, eleven was a winning number when a new game was commencing.

The table went wild as players collected their winnings and put down additional bets. The pile in front of Ron Ryan was even higher now. For an actor begging for a role, he seemed to have a lot of money to back up his play. At least I hoped he did.

Ryan encouraged Mary Ward to continue tossing the dice. Each time she did, the numbers came up seven or eleven, winning for all the players at the table, with the exception of one sullen-looking gentleman in a tuxedo who had decided the odds were against the players, and who was betting *with* the casino, losing on each of Mary's rolls.

After six consecutive winning rolls, she threw a six, which prompted a flurry of betting activity. Now, everyone would win until she "sevened-out." She rolled five consecutive numbers before coming up with the dreaded seven.

It was a happy table. If news of Marla Tralaine's murder had reached everyone, no one in the casino reflected it. The mood was boisterous and upbeat.

"Here," Ryan said, pushing a pile of chips in Mary's direction.

"Oh, no, I couldn't accept that," she said.

"Hey, you were what I thought you'd be—my lucky charm. Buy yourself a pretty dress with it."

She shook her head and said, "That's very generous, Mr. Ryan, but I'm quite content helping you win some money. I won money too, at a slot machine. My friends back home and I will share it. But I think it's time for me to leave. I'm feeling sleepy."

"It's tiring just trying to keep your balance in this storm," someone else at the table said.

Amazing, I thought, how easy it was to forget the roll and pitch of the giant ship when you were focusing on other things. Now that he'd mentioned the storm, I was very much aware of it, and grasped the edge of the craps table to steady myself.

I followed Mary through the throngs of people in the casino. She stopped once at a slot machine, and I saw a twinkle in her eye.

"Don't," I said.

"It is tempting once you've won some money, isn't it?" she said sweetly. "I suppose that's how people become addicted to gambling."

We left the casino and passed the Chart Room, one of three new lounges created during Cunard's $45-million refit, the most extensive refurbishing of the ship in its history. A young man in a tuxedo played popular show tunes on an antique piano.

We stopped, and Mary looked into the bar. "That's the same piano that was on the *Queen Mary*," she said brightly. "I read about it."

"So did I," I said. "It's a lovely lounge, isn't it?"

"Would you like to join me for a nightcap before I go to bed?" she asked.

"That would be nice," I said.

"Nothing alcoholic," she said. "But I'm just not ready to go to my cabin."

"Then let's take that vacant table there."

She ordered a cup of tea; I had club soda with lime.

The music was soothing, although it was disconcerting to see the piano moving in lockstep with the ship's movement. I wondered how difficult it was for the pianist to keep hitting the right notes. I assumed he was used to it.

"Well, Mary," I said, "you've had quite an evening. Ever gambled before?"

"Never at a gambling table like that."

"Maybe you have natural luck," I said. "Mr. Ryan was certainly pleased to have you at his side."

"I suppose he was," she said, sipping her tea. "Funny, but while I was there, I kept thinking back to something I read many years ago."

"Oh? What was that?"

"Poor Ms. Tralaine. To be without clothes and dead in a lifeboat. It makes me shudder just to think of it."

"I know what you mean. It's a grim contemplation. What did being at the craps table remind you of?"

"Do you remember when Ms. Tralaine's husband was murdered in Hollywood?"

"Yes, but not with any clarity. It was in all the headlines, as I recall. I read a few articles about it before coming aboard."

"Yes, it certainly was in the news. I followed the story with some interest. I suppose I have a natural curiosity about such things, like most people. It must have been very difficult for her not only to lose her husband that way, but to be accused of killing him."

"Was she actually accused, or was that just rumor?"

"Oh, no. The authorities at the time were convinced she was behind it. But I suppose they couldn't come up with enough proof, so they dropped that line of inquiry."

"You have a remarkable memory," I said.

"Only about certain things. Other things go right through my brain like a sieve. No, what I remembered while I was standing at that table was a headline that was in one of those dreadful newspapers you see at all the supermarket checkout counters."

"The tabloids," I said.

"Exactly."

"And what was the headline that you recall?"

"Evidently, Ms. Tralaine's husband—I think it was her fourth or fifth—was a very heavy gambler. Some journalists said he had connections to the Mafia in Las Vegas."

"I don't recall any of that," I said. "But I'm listening."

"He was a very big gambler. The headline I remember said, 'Cops Crap Out In Tralaine Case.' "

I laughed. "A colorful headline."

"It certainly was. I can see that front page as clearly today as I did back then."

Where was this leading? I wondered. I waited for her to continue.

"Yes, I can see that front page as though it were on this table in front of me. It had that 'colorful headline' as you say, a picture of Ms. Tralaine's husband being wheeled out of the house on a stretcher and covered with a sheet, a picture of her, and a picture of a man with whom they claimed she was romantically involved."

"And?"

"I think we were standing with that man at the gambling table tonight."

"Who?"

"Mr. Ryan."

"Are you sure?" I asked.

"No. I could never be sure of something like that." She turned, looked at me, and narrowed her pale blue eyes. "But I think I'm right."

I sat back and exhaled, allowing my mind to focus on a few bars of the song being played. It was from one of the popular musicals—*Phantom of the Opera*? I had trouble keeping themes from contemporary musicals straight, although I never have trouble with songs from older shows.

After a few seconds, I returned my attention to what Mary Ward had just told me.

Was she right? Was one of Marla Tralaine's former lovers on board?

If so, that would make two gentlemen from her past present on this crossing when she was murdered—the old actor now functioning as a gentleman escort, and the actor in my play who, I reminded myself, had begged Rip Nestor for the part.

I sat forward again and said, "I think I have some telephone calls to make. I'm going to call someone in New York and see if she'll fax me clippings from when Tralaine's husband was murdered. I assume she can do that using the ship's satellite communication system. I'll ask her to locate the front page of the tabloid you mentioned."

"You'll do that?" she asked. "I wouldn't want to put you to any trouble based upon what might be my faulty memory."

"No, Mary, I think it's very important that I do this. Now, let me tell you about someone *else* on this crossing who goes back a long way with Marla Tralaine."

Chapter Fourteen

We walked to our cabins.

"Have a good sleep," I said.

"You too, Jessica. I'm happy you shared with me what you discovered about that gentleman I danced with."

"It may mean nothing," I said, "but I feel we're ... how shall I put it? ... I feel as though we're in this together. Sort of like partners."

"And I'm very flattered to be considered in that light by someone like you. Will you be at breakfast?"

"Probably, although don't hold me to it. I may eat in my cabin."

"I might do that, too," she said.

"We'll catch up. Good night."

I locked my cabin door behind me and went to the porthole. I don't know whether it was my imagination or not, but the seas seemed to have calmed.

I took the small telephone book I always carry with me from my purse, found the number I was looking for, and called the ship's operator.

"Yes, Mrs. Fletcher?"

"Two things," I said. "First, I need to know how someone back in New York can send me a fax while we're at sea."

"No problem," the operator said, reciting for me the numbers to use.

"Second," I said, "I wish to place a call to New York."

After asking me for the necessary information, the familiar voice of Ruth Lazzara came on the line with remarkable clarity.

"Ruth?"

"Yes?"

"Jessica Fletcher."

"Oh, hi, Jess. What a pleasant surprise."

"I'm calling from the *QE2*."

She laughed. "Why?"

"Why am I calling from the *QE2*?"

"No. Why are you *on* the *QE2*?"

"That's a long story that I will be happy to relate to you at another time. I need a favor, Ruth."

"Sure. Just ask."

Ruth Lazzara was a researcher who worked for a variety of authors, primarily in academic fields, but who also lent her considerable talents to fiction writers like me needing solid factual information for a novel.

"A number of years ago, Ruth, there was a sensational murder case out in Hollywood. Remember the actress, Marla Tralaine?"

"Of course. I read recently that she's negotiating to

make a comeback. A made-for-television movie, I think, for the Teller Network."

"You're absolutely right," I said. "She was . . . she's on the ship."

"That must be interesting. Is she nice?"

"She's . . . she's noncommunicative at the moment."

"Another Marlene?"

"Something like that. One of her former husbands was murdered in Hollywood a while back. It was pretty sensational stuff, was in all the papers."

"I remember that, too, Jess. A huge scandal. Didn't they try to pin the murder on her?"

"I believe they did, although they weren't successful. Ruth, what I need—and I need it yesterday— are some of the clippings about that case. There's one in particular, a supermarket tabloid. I don't know which one. But the entire front page was devoted to the case. It had a picture of her dead husband being wheeled out of their house, a photograph of Marla Tralaine, and another photo of a man purported to be her lover."

There was silence on the other end.

"Ruth?"

"I'm making notes. Sorry. Okay, you want that tabloid story. Others?"

"Send me whatever you can come up with on such short notice."

"But how do I get these to you out in the middle of the ocean?"

"Easy. What a marvelous technological age this is. You can fax them to me." I gave her the information I'd received from the operator about how to fax things to a passenger on the *QE2*. "Keep a record of any expenses. I'll reimburse you the minute I get back."

"The last thing on my mind. Anything else I can do for you?"

"Actually, there is. There's a interesting assortment of people on this trip. I wonder if you could dig up some background on a British actor." I grabbed the video of *Dangerous Woman* I'd watched and scanned the list of credits on the box. "The actor is named Sydney Worrell, Ruth. Never made it big, I presume, but was in a film with Marla Tralaine called *Dangerous Woman*."

"Got it. What else?"

"You mentioned the Teller Network. A number of people who appear on that network are also on this cruise . . . I mean crossing. If you can come up quickly with scuttlebutt having to do with that network, I'd appreciate it. You know, gossip column pieces about Sam Teller and his young wife, Lila Sims. I understand a serious conflict exists between Sam Teller and Marla Tralaine over the film she was to make." I named the other lecturers. "Anything on them, too, that's juicy."

Another laugh from Ruth Lazzara, this time louder and with more meaning. "I didn't know you were a fan of juicy journalism, Jess. I seemed to remember you telling me once that tabloid journalism was boring."

"It is, unless it's wrapped up in real murder."

Her tone turned serious. "Real murder? Has there been a *real* murder on the ship?"

"As a matter of fact, Ruth, there has been. I have a feeling you'll hear all about it tomorrow. Tune in James Brady's television show."

"I hate it when you do this to me, Jess, dangle something in front of me and then leave me guessing."

"Sorry, but I can't do better at the moment. Will you send all this to me?"

"I'll get on it first thing in the morning and shoot the fax to you by the end of the day."

"Great. I knew I could count on you."

"Hey," she said. "You mentioned the movie Marla Tralaine was *going* to make for the Teller Network. Is she—?"

"You're a doll," I said. "I'll be looking for the faxes tomorrow. 'Bye."

That call made, I debated what to do next. My cabin was especially inviting at the moment. Two lamps cast a warm glow over the room, and the gentle rocking of the ship almost made it feel as though I were in a cradle. The thought of climbing into bed and reading a good book until falling asleep was compelling.

On the other hand, I was brimming with energy. I love retiring early, then getting up with the sun. But there are nights when the adrenaline flows, and you just know it would be impossible to fall asleep.

I freshened up, left the cabin, and went to the main staircase, pausing at the Midships Lobby where the history of Samuel Cunard and his remarkable achievements in building this steamship company were depicted. A sprawling four-panel mural by the British artist Peter Sutton traced the history of the line. There were also ship models, artifacts, maritime paintings, and photographs of celebrities from the world of entertainment and politics aboard the ship, all artfully displayed. As I become older, the meaning of history looms more important to me as a measure of who we are, and why we are the way we are.

As I perused the display, other passengers passed on their way to the ship's myriad nighttime activities. I envied them. All they had to think about during the five-day crossing was how to enjoy themselves.

I decided on the spot that I was in for a little enjoyment, too. That morning's program indicated that the editor-in-chief of *Town and Country* magazine, Pamela Fiori, and one of her associates, Michael Cannon, whom I'd heard was a wonderful pianist and singer, were presenting a musical tribute that night to a hundred and fifty years of the magazine. I certainly knew of Ms. Fiori's esteemed reputation in the magazine field, but had no idea she was also musically talented.

The show was being held in the Queens Room, where the tea dance had taken place that afternoon. It sounded like a pleasant diversion from murder, so I headed there, arriving just as the lights dimmed and the show was about to begin. I slipped into an empty chair at a table to the rear of the room. Others at the table didn't pay any attention to me, for which I was grateful.

I was glad I'd decided to catch the show. It was wonderful. Michael Cannon was an immensely talented pianist and singer, and Pam Fiori used a beautifully written narration to link the songs by great American composers to milestones in the magazine's history. The crowd loved it. When the lights came up, the performing duo received a standing ovation, my own applause included in it.

Although many people left the Queens Room after the show, a number stayed for the next round of entertainment, dancing to the *QE2*'s orchestra. I lingered at the table for a few minutes. As I started to leave, James Brady intercepted me. "Hear anything new?" he asked.

I shook my head. "You?"

"No. I tried to confirm how Marla died, but can't get anybody in Security or Medical to open up."

"Have you filed your story yet?" I asked.

"Yes. And I'll be doing a satellite TV feed in the morning. Care to be on with me?"

"Heavens, no, Jim, but thanks for asking." I knew he'd made the North Atlantic crossing on the *QE2* many times before, so I asked, "Have you ever had anything like this happen on your previous crossings?"

"No. Always lots of celebrities aboard, but none of them murdered. Buy you a drink?"

"Yes. I'd like that."

The Queens Grill Lounge was unoccupied, with the exception of a young couple holding hands next to one of the windows. Honeymooners, I judged. The *QE2* always has honeymooning couples aboard. It's an expensive way to celebrate a marriage, but since everything is provided with the exceptions of alcoholic drinks and tips, it averages out to be a pretty good travel value.

We took a table at the opposite end of the room from the young couple. The tiny bar was manned by a charming young Scotsman who took our orders and returned to the bar to prepare them. Hearing his Scottish brogue reminded me of my dear Scottish friend, George Sutherland, a top-ranking inspector for Scotland Yard.

The year before, I'd led a group of friends from Cabot Cove on a trip to Scotland. We stayed in George's family castle in Wick, on the northernmost coast of that magnificent country. Unfortunately, the vacation was marred by murder, a situation that seemed to be following me around these days.

When I told George I was taking the crossing, he expressed disappointment; he wouldn't be in England when I arrived. Something to do with a case in Edinburgh. Seeing him again would, of course, have made the trip that much more enjoyable.

Jim and I toasted each other.

"Having a good time despite tripping over dead bodies?" he asked.

"I think so."

"You don't sound convinced."

"I suppose because I'm not. You?"

"Turning into a real working trip," he replied. "But nothing can ruin a trip for me on the *QE2*. One of my favorite things in the world is to spend five days on this beautiful lady."

"The weather seems to have improved," I said.

"Yes, it has."

"My steward told me we may have a storm bearing down on us."

"Nothing new on the North Atlantic. Oh, by the way, the piece you wrote for the program is very well done."

My eyebrows went up. "How did you know? It's being inserted in *tomorrow's* program."

He gave me a pixieish smile as he pulled a piece of paper from the inside pocket of his tuxedo. "I have a friend."

I shook my head as he handed it to me. "I shouldn't be surprised," I said, "with your connections."

Ms. Jenkins had done a nice job of laying out the five hundred word insert. She hadn't changed a word I'd written. I handed it back to Brady, asking, "Do you think this will allay passenger fears?"

"Not in the least."

We chatted for another half hour about a number of

things, few of them having to do with Marla Tralaine. Finally, he said, "I have to meet up for a drink with one of the British journalists. Walk you back to your cabin?"

"No, but thanks for offering. I think I'll just sit here a while. I'm not quite ready for bed."

He gave the bartender his gold Cunard card, signed the receipt, said good-bye, and left.

I declined the bartender's offer of another drink; I'd only sipped the first one, and most of it was left in the glass. I closed my eyes and focused upon the movement of the ship. It just keeps going, I thought, thirty knots, relentlessly pressing forward no matter what events take place onboard, eighteen hundred men, women, and children enjoying themselves on what was undoubtedly for many the trip of a lifetime, as it had been for Frank and me twenty years ago.

Thinking of my late husband made me sad; it was time to go to my cabin and call it a night.

As I got up from the table and started to leave, the door leading up to the penthouse area opened and a man stepped past it. I didn't recognize him for a moment, then saw it was Jerry Lackman, the actor playing Billy Bravo, the detective in my play. He looked at me. I waved. He immediately turned and left the lounge, leaving no doubt in my mind that seeing me had caused him to bolt.

I opened the door leading up to the penthouse

suites and ascended the stairs. I paused in the carpeted hallway. Directly in front of me was the small
kitchen area in which Mr. Montrose, the gentleman's
gentleman, prepared drinks and snacks for passengers
staying on that level. He stepped from behind a partition and said, "May I help you, ma'am?"

"I'm Jessica Fletcher," I said.

He smiled. "Yes, ma'am, I am aware of that."

"I . . . I was supposed to meet Mr. Lackman here.
He's one of the actors in my play."

"I'm afraid you've missed him, Mrs. Fletcher. He
just left Mr. Teller's penthouse."

"He left Mr. Teller's penthouse?"

"Yes, ma'am. Only a minute or so ago."

"I see," I said. "Well, I suppose I'll catch up with
him elsewhere on the ship."

As I was about to go down the stairs, another person stepped from behind the partition. I recognized
him instantly from photographs I'd seen in newspapers, and from news programs on television. It was
Samuel Teller, founder and chairman of the Teller
Cable Network. He directed his glare first at me, then
at Mr. Montrose.

"Thank you," I said. "Have a pleasant evening."

Teller's hard stare stayed with me all the way back
to my cabin. Once there, I pulled a notebook and pen
from my bag, sat in one of the club chairs beneath the
porthole, and started to write.

Marla Tralaine murdered. Cause of death unknown. Naked body found in lifeboat on Boat Deck.

Tralaine connected with many people on the ship. Old British actor from early movie signs on this particular crossing to work as gentleman host.

Former lover during period her husband murdered years ago begs for a role in theatrical production on this particular crossing.

Bad blood between Teller Network founder Sam Teller and Tralaine, presumably over movie she was to make for him.

Mary Ward smells garlic in Tralaine's penthouse. TV chef Carlo Di Giovanni reeks of garlic from cooking.

One rumored cause of death, according to James Brady, is a pick of some sort, perhaps used by mountain climbers. Lecturer Troy Radcliff, world-famous mountain climber, is aboard.

Another rumored cause of death is poison. Plant expert Elaine Ananthous is to give lecture on poison plants, and how they've been used in murder mysteries.

Tralaine's hairdresser, Candy Malone, knew of the murder almost immediately that morning. How did she hear about it so fast?

Tralaine's manager, Peter Kunz, was on Boat Deck the morning Mary Ward and I discovered body.

Mary Ward points out it would take a strong person to hoist Tralaine's dead body up into lifeboat. Tralaine's personal trainer, Tony Silvestrie, would certainly qualify in that regard.

I stopped, pondered other possible connections, and resumed writing.

During lunch with director Rip Nestor he referred to Marla Tralaine as a "bitch." Why? Was he responding only to her public reputation? Or had he known her personally?

Troy Radcliff and Marla Tralaine shared a dislike for pineapple. Hardly worthy of noting, but might as well.

Rip Nestor's director's copy of my script, with all his notes written on it, was found in Marla Tralaine's penthouse. Why?

Now, the most recent possible connection came to mind.

Actor Jerry Lackman, playing my detective hero, Billy Bravo, is seen coming from penthouse area. Mr. Montrose, butler to penthouse passengers, tells me Lackman had come from the penthouse occupied by cable TV mogul Sam Teller and his young actress wife, Lila Sims. Why would this actor be meeting with Sam Teller? Mary Ward thinks Lackman is from Los Angeles based upon his accent, although he claims to be a New Yorker. Lackman urged me to introduce him to Marla Tralaine. When Lackman told me he knew about the murder, he said he got it through "official channels." Why would this actor be in the official loop?

Whenever I find myself personally involved in murder, I always find it useful to make a list such as the one I'd just written. It helps keep my thoughts focused, and puts people and things into perspective.

I couldn't think of anything else to write, so I put the pad and pen on the cocktail table, went to the closet, took out a nightgown, carefully hung up the evening wear I'd had on, slipped into the nightgown, added a robe and slippers, and went to the bathroom to brush my teeth. I'd just taken the cap off the toothpaste when my phone rang. Who would be calling me at this hour?

I returned to the bedroom and picked up the receiver.

"Jessica?"

I recognized his voice immediately. It was my dear friend George Sutherland.

"George? Why are you calling me?"

"I'm offended," he said, his brogue coming through. "Do I have to have a reason?"

"No, of course not. I'm sorry. It's just that it's been a hectic day and night and—"

"Aside from always enjoying talking to you, Jessica, there is another reason for my call."

"Where are you calling from?"

"London."

"I thought you were in Edinburgh."

"I was, but I was called back. It seems you've had a nasty incident aboard the *QE2*."

"That's putting it mildly. You've heard?"

"Oh, yes. The ship contacted The Yard, and they brought me back to London to coordinate the investigation from this end."

"You'll be investigating Marla Tralaine's murder?"

"Afraid so. The plan is for us to dispatch a helicopter from Southampton as soon as the ship comes within range of the aircraft. I'll be on board along with forensic experts."

"Flying out to the *QE2* on a helicopter? Have you ever done that before?"

He laughed. "No, can't say that I have. But isn't that what's enjoyable about being alive? Something new every day."

"I suppose so, although I wish the reason for it weren't the murder of a famous actress."

"Quite so," he said. "My information is that you discovered the body, poor dear."

"In reality, a lovely woman I've befriended actually spotted the very dead Ms. Tralaine."

"Anything you can tell me that might help in my planning?"

"You mean suspects, clues, things like that?"

"Exactly. I know you only too well, Jessica Fletcher. When a murder takes place in your general vicinity, you usually end up to your pretty neck in it."

"A terrible reputation to bear. As a matter of fact, I just finished making notes on what's occurred so far."

"Splendid. Read them to me."

"Hold on."

After I'd gone through my notes with him, he said, "You've been a very busy girl."

"Too busy, I'm afraid. There really hasn't been time to enjoy this wonderful experience. But I'm determined I eventually will." I mentioned that I'd been called upon to write the insert for the morning's program.

"Read that to me, too, if you will," he said.

"I can't. I don't have it with me," I replied, wishing I'd kept the copy Jim Brady had shown me.

"I wish you weren't so directly involved," George said.

"Too late for that now, George. No telling what tomorrow will bring, so I think I ought to get to bed."

"And I won't keep you from that."

"Do you know what, George?"

"What?"

"There is one good thing to come out of this."

"Which is?"

"The change in your plans. It means I'll have a chance to see you."

"Right you are, Jessica. Murder can have its advantages."

"I didn't quite mean that."

"Nor did I. Go on, get your beauty sleep. But let's stay in touch until I get there. I'll call tomorrow."

I glanced at my watch, which I'd set ahead an hour upon instruction in that day's program. When crossing the Atlantic, passengers are told to turn their watches ahead an hour each day so that when they reach England, the time change has been accounted for, and there's less disturbance of circadian rhythms, also known as jet lag.

"It's already tomorrow."

"Sleep tight, Jessica. Speak with you again in a few hours."

Chapter Fifteen

Although I'd gone to bed late, I slept fitfully, and was awake to hear that day's program being slipped beneath my door at five A.M. I hurriedly got out of bed, picked up the newsletter, and opened to the inserted announcement of Marla Tralaine's death.

My reaction to seeing it was not one of pleasure or pride. Becoming the *QE2*'s temporary spokesperson for this tragedy sounded logical at the time it was presented to me. But I now sensed that Security Chief Prall and the others had played upon my ego, which I like to think is generally intact. I'm not easily flattered.

Yes, I bought the rationale at the time that having someone like me act as the unified voice for the eighteen hundred other passengers would be a positive thing.

But for whom?

In the harsh reality of morning, I realized it wouldn't be me.

I showered quickly, dressed casually for the day,

and dealt with the decision of whether to have breakfast in my cabin or in the Queens Grill. There was the strong temptation to remain in seclusion, perhaps for the duration of the trip to avoid the inevitable questions that would be asked of me by other passengers who'd read the announcement. But I knew I couldn't do that—*wouldn't* do that—because it would cheat me out of enjoying the rest of the crossing.

As I opened my door, my steward, Walter, passed with a breakfast tray for another cabin. He stopped and said, "Good morning, Mrs. Fletcher. Sleep well?"

"To be truthful, no."

"I read what you wrote about Ms. Tralaine," he said. "But I knew about it before that."

"I'm sure you did. Word gets around pretty quickly when somebody's murdered."

He hesitated before asking, "Do you know who killed her, Mrs. Fletcher?"

"No. And frankly, Walter, I'd just as soon not know."

"The crew has ideas about it."

"I'm sure they do. Everyone on the ship is probably speculating. The little thing I wrote was intended to head off such speculation. I'm afraid it won't."

"Well, I'd better deliver this breakfast before it gets cold," he said. "I don't know what's wrong with people these days, shooting a beautiful lady like that." He started to walk away.

"Walter."

"Yes, ma'am?"

"You said *shooting* someone. Was Ms. Tralaine *shot*?"

He shrugged. "That's what some of the stewards say. Excuse me, ma'am. Have a nice day."

I was stopped twice on my way to breakfast. An elderly couple saw me going up the main staircase. "Mrs. Fletcher, we recognize you from your picture on your books. We have them all," said the wife.

"That's nice to hear."

"We read what you wrote this morning in the program," said the husband. "My God, it's really true. There was a rumor that something had happened to Ms. Tralaine, but now you've made it official. Who could have done such a thing?"

"I have no idea," I said. "London's Scotland Yard has been informed. They'll fly in to investigate when we're closer to land."

"Not soon enough for me," said the wife. "Dreadful, having a dead body on board. We saved for years for this trip."

"Don't let it spoil your crossing," I said. "The captain and his crew have everything under control."

My second interception came just as I was about to go through the entrance to the Queens Lounge on my way to the Grill. This time, it was one of the British journalists traveling in a group from New York to England.

"Hamish Monroe," he said, shaking my hand. He was a young man, no more than thirty, with pink cheeks and large brown eyes. He pulled a reporter's notebook from the inside pocket of his brown tweed jacket, held a pen in the other hand, and asked, "Would you tell me the circumstances under which you found Marla Tralaine's body?"

"I didn't find her body," I said.

"But you indicated in the program this morning that you had."

"It was a bit of a misstatement," I said. "I was with the person who discovered the body. But I personally didn't see it until it was pointed out to me."

He wrote in his pad, looked up, and asked, "Who was the individual who actually first saw her body?"

"Another passenger," I said. "Mrs. Ward."

"Ward? Is she traveling with you?"

"No."

I should not have given out Mary Ward's name. Too late now.

"What is this Mrs. Ward's first name?" he asked.

My stomach growled. "You'll have to excuse me, Mr. Monroe. I'm late for breakfast. I'm meeting people."

"Mind if I join you?"

"For breakfast? You look like you're leaving the restaurant."

"A cup of coffee then?" He asked it pleasantly; his smile was genuine.

"Mr. Monroe," I said, "I'd just as soon not have to deal with the press at breakfast, and I'm sure my friends

149

feel the same way. Could we meet at another time? Just the two of us?"

"Splendid," he said. "Your cabin in, say, an hour?"

"Why don't you call me later this morning and we'll arrange something."

As I entered the dining room and received my usual expansive greeting from the maitre d', I glanced over at my table where the TV chef, Carlo Di Giovanni, sat across from television's plant lady, Elaine Ananthous. Judging from the angry expressions on their faces, they weren't happy to be together.

I hesitated before approaching them, and further observed. My initial instinct was obviously correct. Ananthous started to cry as Di Giovanni leaned across the table and spoke in a loud, angry voice. Maybe I'd better get there, I thought, to act as mediator.

As I approached, Di Giovanni stopped speaking and sat back in his chair, his face an angry mask. Elaine dabbed at her eyes with her napkin and turned away from me.

"Good morning," I said cheerily, hoping to inject some pleasantness into the atmosphere. "Have you eaten yet?"

"No," Di Giovanni mumbled.

"Good. I hate to eat alone." I slipped into the chair Jacques pulled out for me. He hovered there. "I'm hungry this morning," I told him. "We have wonderful blueberry pancakes back in Maine, and I find myself yearning for them this morning. Would the chef make me a stack of blueberry pancakes?"

"Of course," he replied.

"And two strips of bacon, well done. Orange juice and coffee."

We sat in silence until I said, "I have the feeling you two have had a professional spat. Care to tell me about it?"

Di Giovanni responded by standing, throwing his napkin on the table, and saying, "This woman is impossible. I will eat elsewhere."

We watched him leave, his steps heavy and deliberate. I turned to Elaine. "You've been crying," I said. "Is there something I can do?"

"I hate that man," she said in her birdlike, singsong voice, running her fingers through her thinning hair.

"He is a little volatile," I said, adding a laugh to soften things. "But he seems nice enough."

She leaned closer to me. "Do you know what he's been trying to do to me at the network?" she asked in a stage whisper.

"No."

"He's been trying for months to get my show canceled."

"Why would he do that?"

"Because he has an Italian friend who's a florist. He wants management to get rid of me and give the show to his friend."

"Sometimes there's a misunderstanding about those

things. Are you sure he's personally trying to have you taken off the air?"

"Yes, I am. He's a vile, evil, wicked man. He told me just before you arrived that he's meeting about it with Mr. Teller this afternoon."

I didn't know what my reaction should be, so I said, "I've watched you on television, Elaine. I love your show. You certainly know a great deal about plants and flowers."

"Of course I do. I've been studying horticulture for years. My ratings are good, and the show gets lots of mail. Mr. Teller wouldn't take me off the air with good ratings and with all that mail, would he?"

"I don't know Sam Teller, Elaine, except from what I've read in the newspapers."

"I tried to call him in his cabin this morning. He's not taking any calls. At least he's not taking *my* calls."

"He must be a very busy man."

"Do you think he would listen to you, Jessica?"

"I can't imagine why he would."

She became animated. "Would you talk to Sam Teller about this situation? Put in a good word for me?"

"If I have the opportunity."

She appeared to be somewhat relieved. "I just know he'd listen to someone of your stature," she said. "He'd have to. He'd probably like to make movies of your books for the network. Yes, I've heard that he was thinking of doing that. Oh, please, Jessica, show

him how wrong it would be to take me off the air."
She grasped my forearm and squeezed.

Jacques arrived with my breakfast, and not too soon.
I was becoming uncomfortable with the conversation.

"Still planning to speak on the use of poisonous
plants in murder mysteries?" I asked between bites.

"I suppose so. That's what I came prepared to do. I
might as well go through with it, although I don't know
how I possibly can, considering everything that's happened to me, Marla Tralaine's murder, and that dis-
gusting chef threatening me."

I was tempted to ask how Marla Tralaine's murder
impacted negatively upon her, but didn't. She was
obviously distraught. Better to let her vent, and stay
out of the way.

I promised her I'd show up to hear her lecture, which
seemed to please her. She left the table to get ready, and
I lingered over a second cup of coffee. The dining room
had begun to fill up; other passengers approached the
table to ask me about Marla Tralaine's murder. I tried to
be as gracious as possible, although I found myself
becoming annoyed at yet another intrusion into my
quiet time. I left the dining room as soon as it was convenient and headed for the Boat Deck where, weather
permitting, I'd take a brisk walk to counter my heavy
breakfast.

I stopped in the Queens Lounge to peer out the window. I couldn't believe my eyes. The sun was shining, a
welcome sight.

As I stood on the Boat Deck and took deep breaths of the refreshing ocean air, Sandy, the young man who'd led me to my cabin when I boarded in New York, came up to me. "I just want you to know, Mrs. Fletcher, how much we appreciate you writing that insert for the program. I think it has put many passengers' minds to rest."

"That was the intention," I replied, "although I'm not sure it will accomplish anything."

"I think it will. There was a growing restlessness. Perhaps this will calm things down."

"What I'm delighted about is this change in weather," I said. "How lovely to see the sun again."

"I hate to be a wet blanket, Mrs. Fletcher, but it's only a brief respite from the foul weather we've been having. The bridge has been tracking a North Atlantic storm since leaving New York. Forecast was that it would veer away. But it's taken a sudden turn and is bearing down directly on us."

"Can't we change course?" I asked.

"From what I hear, there isn't time for that," he said. "But not to worry. This grand old lady of the sea can ride through any storm. I was aboard last year when that monster wave hit us."

"I vaguely remember reading something about that."

"Oh, yes. Almost a hundred feet high. Came right up to the bridge."

"Must have been frightening for passengers," I said, mentally placing myself into the situation.

"Most didn't even know about it. It hit us at two in the morning. The passengers slept right through it. Only minor damage."

"Well," I said, "that certainly confirms what you've said about the seaworthiness of this ship. Glad to hear it."

"About to take a walk?" he asked.

"Yes. I'd better take advantage of this 'brief respite,' as you put it."

As I walked, I realized this was only the second full day on the *QE2*. It would all be over so fast, this marvelous five days at sea. I'd heard that Cunard intended to extend future *QE2* Atlantic crossings to six days in order to provide an extra day for passengers, as well as to give the captain more time to make course corrections in the event of inclement weather. Whatever the reason, I was all for a longer journey.

When I approached the lifeboat where we'd discovered Marla Tralaine's body, I looked away and picked up the pace.

I'd just completed one full turn about the deck when Priscilla Warren, my assigned guide for the crossing, stepped onto the deck from an inside hallway and said, "Mrs. Fletcher, I've been looking for you."

"Well, you found me, Priscilla. What can I do for you?"

"You've been getting a series of calls. Here."

She handed me a dozen message slips. George Sutherland had called from London. My Cabot Cove friends, Seth Hazlitt and Mort Metzger, had left messages asking me to return their calls. And there were nine messages from passengers, including the British journalist I'd briefly chatted with that morning, Hamish Monroe.

"Do I have to return all these passenger calls?" I asked.

"Up to you, Mrs. Fletcher. The cruise director simply felt we ought to get these to you straightaway in the event some of them were important."

"I appreciate that. I think what I'll do is take a couple more turns around the deck before going back to my cabin."

I did two more laps, message slips in hand, before returning inside. I was on the Midships Staircase when Security Chief Prall came bounding up from below. "Mrs. Fletcher, glad to have caught up with you. A word?"

I sighed. My intention to cross the North Atlantic curled up with a good book was obviously wishful thinking.

"Mrs. Fletcher," he said, gravity in his voice, "two of our passengers are spreading the story that Scotland Yard is going to be flying a helicopter in here to investigate the murder of Ms. Tralaine."

"Really?" I said.

"Yes. They said you were the one who informed them of it."

"I did?"

"My question is, how did *you* find out?"

"I—"

"Our communication with Scotland Yard in London was on a secured line."

"Was it?"

I'd made my indiscreet comment about Scotland Yard to two passengers earlier that morning, and was wrong in having done it. I'd heard it directly from the proverbial horse's mouth, George Sutherland, who was to be in charge of the investigation, and I had no right telling anyone else. I thought back to a line from a blues song written by a pianist and singer I enjoy, Mose Allison: "Your mind is on vacation, your mouth is working overtime." Better keep your mind *and* mouth on vacation from now on, I silently admonished myself.

"If I did say something like that, Mr. Prall, all I can say is I'm sorry. It won't happen again."

He shook his head and pursed his lips before saying, "Mrs. Fletcher, that's not the point. How did you know Scotland Yard would be sending a helicopter here once we're within flying range of Southampton?"

"I suppose it just makes sense to me for that to happen," I said, getting deeper into my lie. I've always avoided lying because liars have such trouble remembering what lies they've told. By the same token, I didn't want to reveal my relationship with George Sutherland. So I said, "Obviously, as good as security is on this ship, you don't have the forensic personnel to properly investigate a murder. But someone is going to have to do it, some official law enforcement body. And

157

since we're sailing to England, it just makes sense that it would be Scotland Yard fulfilling that responsibility."

He looked as though he wasn't sure whether to accept my explanation. But then he said, "I don't read a lot of murder mysteries, Mrs. Fletcher, so I'm not familiar with the way a mystery writer's mind works. I suppose if you were writing a book about this, you'd have Scotland Yard fly to the ship and take over the investigation."

"Yes," I said brightly, "that's exactly right. If I were writing a book about this, that is precisely what I would write."

"All I can ask is that you not repeat this fictional scenario to anyone else. It's misleading, if you know what I mean."

"I certainly do, Mr. Prall. Sorry to have caused you any problem."

I went to my cabin and returned George Sutherland's call. He was out of the office and wouldn't be back for hours.

I checked my watch and saw that there was only a half hour until Elaine Ananthous's lecture in the Grand Lounge. I decided to put off returning the other calls until later. But as I was about to leave, the phone rang.

"Jessica?"

"Yes."

"James Brady."

"Yes, Jim. How are you?"

"Great. What's this about Scotland Yard flying to the ship to investigate Tralaine's murder?"

"Sounds like the overly active imagination of a mystery writer."

"Any mystery writer I'd know?"

"Can I talk to you later, Jim? I have to return some calls, and I'm due at a lecture."

"Sure. Want to be a guest on my satellite feed at noon?"

"Goodness, no. But if I get a chance, I'll pop up and watch. Where are you broadcasting from?"

"The Helicopter Deck. Nice break in the weather."

"Lovely day, although they say it might change. Noon on the Helicopter Deck, you say? I'll be there."

The crowd for Elaine Ananthous's lecture was sparse. I spotted Mary Ward sitting alone at a table and joined her. "Breakfast in your room this morning?" I asked.

"Yes. It's such an indulgence."

I laughed and said, "There's an old saying, Mary. 'Living well is the best revenge.' "

She looked at me with wide eyes. "But I don't have anyone I seek revenge against."

"Just a saying, that's all," I said as Priscilla Warren came to the microphone to introduce Elaine. Before she did, she said, "As you know if you've read your program this morning, the famed television chef Carlo Di Giovanni will be giving a cooking demonstration right here this afternoon following Act Two of the murder mystery play. He's been gracious enough to offer to cook a gourmet meal for one special passenger. We've pulled a cabin number from the hat, so to speak, to come up with the winner. And she is—Mrs. Mary Alice Ward." There was a smattering of applause.

"Mary, that's wonderful," I said.

"This must be my lucky year," she said. "Winning this crossing, and now a gourmet meal by a famous chef."

"Just as long as you like garlic."

"I think I can get used to it."

A table set up next to the microphone contained a variety of plants. Elaine tentatively approached the mike, eyes darting left and right, her facial tic visible even from where we sat.

Her lecture was, to be kind, painful. She spoke so softly she could barely be heard. Worse, she seemed perpetually confused. The small audience soon became smaller as people wandered away. By the time she was finished and asked if anyone had questions, no more than two dozen people remained, including me and Mary Ward.

She came to our table and sat heavily for such a small woman. "I just knew it was going to be awful," she said, wringing her hands. "My God, it was excruciating being up there." She sat up straighter and took in the large lounge. "Look. Everyone left. They hated it. It's bound to get back to Sam Teller. He'll use it as an excuse to fire me."

"I thought it was very interesting," Mary Ward said. "Very interesting, indeed."

I said, "Elaine, stop worrying so much about Sam Teller. I'm sure he won't have any idea that the audience was not as big as you would have liked it to be. And Mary is right. It *was* interesting."

"But I was so nervous. I'm supposed to be a television star. Did I look like a television star up there?"

"It doesn't matter," I said.

But she wouldn't be dissuaded from her grim post-mortem of her performance. "It's all because of that rotten man, Di Giovanni. He deliberately upset me this morning because he wanted me to fall on my face. I hate him. I really and truly hate him."

She took in the lounge again. "Wasn't Troy here?"

"Troy Radcliff?" I said. "No, I didn't see him."

"He promised he'd be here. He's such a good man, you know. He really is quite fond of my show. I know he'll go to bat for me with Teller if he tries to get rid of me. I hope he isn't sick. He's getting on in years."

"Yes, I noticed" I said. "But we should all be in such wonderful physical condition at his age."

"I'll go call his cabin," she said, standing and straightening her shapeless gray dress.

Because we both looked up at her, our vision also took in the shopping promenade one deck above.

"Look," Mary Ward said, "that's the actress, Lila Sims."

Elaine looked up, too. "Sam Teller's bimbo wife," she said, lip curled, her voice a snarl.

"Who is that with her?" Mary asked.

"That's . . . that *was* Ms. Tralaine's personal trainer, Mr. Silvestrie," I said.

"He's trying to get his own show on the network," Elaine Ananthous said. "Physical fitness. I'm sure he'd like to get rid of me, too, and use my half hour for his own stupid program."

Passengers on the promenade also recognized Lila Sims. One asked for her autograph. She was not a big star, but had made a name for herself appearing in B movies in which she played sexy young female characters, her on-screen wardrobe consisting primarily of bikini swimsuits. The passenger asking for the autograph was young, a teenager. As he held up pad and pen, Silvestrie pushed him aside, took Sims by the arm, and hurried her away.

"Hardly the way to please your fans," I said, disgusted with that sort of behavior from a public person.

"He's probably just trying to protect her, considering what happened to the other actress on the ship," Mary Ward offered. She seemed always to see the good in people, to find a reasonable explanation for bad behavior.

Ananthous left us to call Troy Radcliff's cabin, and Mary Ward and I departed the Grand Lounge in the opposite direction.

"I took a walk on the Boat Deck this morning," I said. "I missed your company."

"And I missed my early morning exercise," she said. "I'll be sure to make up for it tomorrow."

"Good. I'll join you. In case we don't see each other for the rest of the day, shall we make it seven tomorrow? On the Boat Deck?"

"Yes," she said. "I look forward to it."

I whiled away the hour before James Brady's satellite feed by sitting in a deck chair where a young deck steward wrapped me in a thick red blanket and brought me a steaming cup of bouillon. Frank and I had done this every day during our crossing twenty years ago, and the forty-five minutes represented the first true moment of peace and tranquility I'd experienced since boarding.

Soak up every blessed minute of it, Jess, I told myself. You may not have many more moments like it.

Chapter Sixteen

James Brady's satellite feed represented an impressive exclusive for his network. With the sun shining and a stiff breeze causing his yellow necktie to flap, he stood in front of a huge camera and assorted supporting electronic gear supplied by the ship's communications department, and told of Marla Tralaine's murder, stressing that the cause of death had not been released by shipboard medical personnel. He mentioned the names of others traveling with her—her personal manager, Peter Kunz, her hairdresser, Candy Malone, and her personal trainer, Tony Silvestrie—and also reported that the founder and chairman of the Teller Cable Network, Sam Teller, and his actress wife, Lila Sims, were aboard. Before ending his report, he glanced over at me, then faced the camera again, and said, "And America's most famous mystery writer, Jessica Fletcher, is here with us, perhaps poised to solve this murder before we reach Southampton. This is James Brady reporting from the North Atlantic on the beautiful *QE2*, which unfortunately is also the scene of controversial actress Marla Tralaine's murder."

"How was it?" he asked.

"Sounded good to me. You're the only television commentator with the story. As they say, timing is everything."

He laughed. "Have you learned anything new this morning?"

"No."

"Anything new about Scotland Yard flying to the ship in a couple of days?"

"No," I said. I would have been happy to share the information with him because not only had he been a friend for years, but his reputation as a journalist was pristine. But I couldn't betray the confidence George Sutherland had placed in me, so I added nothing.

Because my next lecture wasn't scheduled until the following day, the afternoon promised to be a more tranquil one than yesterday. I would, of course, attend Act Two of the play, and was determined to again enjoy the tea dance. TV chef Carlo Di Giovanni was to give his lecture and cooking demonstration at five, with Mary Ward as his special dinner guest.

I wasn't hungry after my sizable breakfast and would have preferred eating lunch at the last possible minute. But that would mean missing the beginning of Act Two. I opted to skip the Queens Grill, going instead to The Pavilion, at the stern of the ship just off the One Deck swimming pool, where meals are served cafeteria-style, including light fare. A lot of other passengers evidently were in the same mood, because the lines were long. But they moved quickly, and I eventually found a table for my grilled chicken Caesar salad and cup of tea.

Although a few passengers stopped by to say hello, only one asked anything about my insert in that day's program. He wanted to know whether there was any truth to the rumor that Marla Tralaine's body was to be buried at sea. I said I hadn't heard anything about that, adding that I doubted it since her death was not from natural causes, and a full investigation would have to be launched once we got to England.

What rumor would be next? That she'd risen from the dead and was seeking revenge on her killer? I wouldn't have been surprised.

The Grand Lounge was standing room only when I arrived at two, and dozens of onlookers leaned on the railing of the shopping promenade above. I was, of course, delighted that the play I'd written had attracted so many interested passengers. But I also wondered whether the news of Marla Tralaine's murder, now public knowledge because of the insert I'd written, had attracted the curious who would not have been there otherwise.

Director Rip Nestor bounced out to the microphone, welcomed everyone to Act Two of the shipboard murder mystery, and briefly brought the audience up to speed on what had occurred the previous day. I glanced around in search of my fellow lecturers. The only one I saw was Judge Dan Solon, sitting with people he'd been with at the craps table last night.

Nestor completed his recap. He then said, "The New York Police Department has sent one of its top investigators to the scene in an attempt to unravel the murder of Millard Wainscott. The man is a legend in criminal investigation. Please welcome Detective Billy Bravo."

Jerry Lackman, the actor playing Detective Bravo, swaggered onto the stage. He wore a holster beneath his left arm in which a snub-nosed revolver was nestled. A portable radio hung from his belt, and he carried a pad and pen. I watched with interest as he took the lines I'd written and used them only as a blueprint for his ad-lib presentation to the audience. He did the same while questioning the other actors and actresses playing the parts of employees at the TV studio. Because I had seen the two videos of other shows produced by Malibu Mysteries, I'd deliberately created situations in which Detective Bravo could use the names and a few facts about certain passengers in the audience, and drew them into the plot as potential suspects. He was brilliant in the way he handled the audience. I was very impressed.

I thought back to Mary Ward's comment that he

sounded to her as though he came from California, not New York; I had to agree with her. Lackman did not have an accent that even hinted of native New Yorker. Did that matter? I wondered. Was there some meaning I should assign to it in terms of Marla Tralaine's death? If there was, I couldn't come up with it at the moment.

But then I also thought of Lackman's telling me he'd learned of the murder through "official channels." And, why had he been visiting Sam Teller in the cable network owner's penthouse suite?

I didn't linger on these questions because I became caught up in the stage action. I've always thought that writing a play must be the most rewarding of all literary efforts because you get to see what you've written played back in an immediate setting. Great playwrights must gain a tremendous psychic satisfaction from seeing their efforts performed night after night, with skilled actors and actresses interpreting the characters they'd created. Of course, the play being performed on the *QE2* would hardly rank as great theater. But I was satisfied.

As Act Two neared its conclusion, I anxiously waited for the second murder to occur. It wouldn't surprise, me, of course. But I hoped it would shock the audience.

It happened with such suddenness that even I was taken by surprise. A young woman suddenly stepped from behind a screen, a knife in her hand. She took a few steps toward the character, John Craig, the TV studio's floor director played by the handsome black actor, John Johnson.

"What the hell are you doing here?" Johnson asked.

"To do this," she responded, raising the knife high above her head and plunging it into his chest, the blade on the specially constructed stage prop disappeared into the handle, making it appear that it had entered deep into his body.

The girl disappeared. It had happened so fast that it was doubtful anyone could describe what she looked like.

Johnson, the actor, clutched his chest and stumbled forward to the stage apron. Red theatrical blood oozed from behind his hands as they clutched at his wound. He fell to his knees. His eyes opened wide. So did his mouth, but no words came.

He tumbled over onto his back.

Detective Billy Bravo had been off-stage when the second murder took place. He reappeared, gazed at the body on the floor, looked out into the audience, and said with theatrical flourish, "Very interesting. Now, two people are dead. And I think there are some suspects sitting here who need to answer some tough questions."

He called on four audience members by name, causing them to giggle. When each stood, he asked them a series of questions about a relationship they might have had with the floor director, John Craig. It all went smoothly, and there was much laughter. When

Bravo walked with purpose from the stage, a determined look on his face, the audience jumped to its feet and applauded long and loud. This was better than I'd ever hoped it would be when I sat in my house in Cabot Cove, the snow swirling around outside my window, and wrote the scene.

A number of people stopped by to congratulate me. Judge Dan Solon, whose gruff style had been off-putting ever since we'd first met, offered a surprisingly warm comment, which I graciously accepted. The *QE2*'s cruise director told me how much wonderful feedback the play was generating. And I was pleased to see Mary Ward approach from a far corner.

"That was wonderful," she said.

"Thank you, Mary. Are you all set for your special gourmet dinner with Mr. Di Giovanni?"

"I think so. I just hope what he prepares isn't too heavy."

"I'm sure he'll whip up something to your liking. Going to the tea dance?"

She waited for others to leave before answering my question. "I certainly intend to," she said. "I'm interested in seeing that man again you say was in one of Ms. Tralaine's early films."

"I'm interested in seeing him again, too," I said. "I'm considering being direct with him, telling him that I know of his previous career as an actor."

"Do you think that's wise?" she asked, frowning.

"I don't know," I said. "I'll have to play it by ear.

You have your dinner with Di Giovanni right after the tea dance, don't you?"

"Would you mind if I skipped going with you to the dance?" she asked. "I think I'll rest a little before my big culinary event."

I laughed. "That sounds like a good idea. Whatever I decide to do with our favorite gentleman host, I'll let you know later."

"By the way, Jessica, did you receive the material from your friend back in New York?"

"Not yet, and I'm glad you reminded me. I'd better alert the communications office that I'm expecting faxes from the States. Enjoy your rest."

I decided to spend some time in my cabin, too, before the tea dance. As I headed there, Peter Kunz, Marla Tralaine's manager, joined me.

"Have a minute, Mrs. Fletcher?" he asked.

"That depends," I said. "I was hoping for a quiet hour before the tea dance."

"It won't take long," he said. "There's someone who would like to spend a few minutes with you."

I stopped. So did he. I looked at him and asked, "And who might that be?"

"Sam Teller, chairman of the Teller Cable Network."

"Why would he want to see me?"

"I don't know. He asked me to find you and bring you up to his penthouse. That is, if you're not too busy."

The real question I had was why Sam Teller would

dispatch Marla Tralaine's manager to bring me to his penthouse. I asked.

Kunz smiled. He was a handsome young man, dressed this afternoon in a double-breasted blue blazer with gold buttons, white shirt, blue-and-red tie with a nautical motif, and white slacks with a knife-edge crease. "Marla and Sam Teller were in negotiations for her to do two movies for his network," he said as we resumed walking. "As her manager, I was intimately involved with the talks. Now that she's dead, I'm developing other projects with Mr. Teller. We've been huddling during the crossing. Will you come meet him? I'm sure it won't take more than ten minutes."

"All right."

I followed Kunz up the stairs from the Queens Lounge to the penthouse level where the personal butler to its passengers, Mr. Montrose, stood proudly in his small kitchen, preparing a tray of snacks and drinks. Kunz ignored him and headed down the hall in the direction of Teller's penthouse. But I greeted the butler, and he returned my greeting. He had an expression on his face that almost said to me that there was something important he wanted to say, but wouldn't. Or couldn't.

I didn't have time to dwell on it because Kunz had already reached the door and knocked. The door opened and Samuel Teller, head of one of the country's most powerful media conglomerates, stood in the doorway. Although I had seen many pictures of him over the years, I didn't realize how big he was, almost filling the space created by the open door. A thick head of battleship gray hair was perfectly shaped to his strong, square, tanned face. He wore a short Chinese red silk smoking jacket secured around his waist with a sash. His eyes were green, the color of Granny Smith apples.

"Mrs. Fletcher, I'm Sam Teller." He extended a large, strong hand, which I took.

"Please, come in," he said, stepping back to allow me to enter. As I did, he said, "It was good of you to come up here on such short notice."

Kunz started to enter, too, but Teller told him, "Come back in a half hour."

Teller closed the door, and we were alone, unless his wife, the young actress Lila Sims, was somewhere in the suite.

He crossed the large room to the sliding doors leading to one of his two balconies, turned, and said, "Drink?"

"No, thank you. This is a lovely penthouse."

"We like it. Coffee? Cup of tea? Soft drink?"

I smiled. "None of the above. I told Mr. Kunz that I was anxious to get to my cabin for a little private time before the tea dance. He said you were anxious to speak with me. About what?"

Teller answered by pointing to a couch. "Please, sit there," he said.

He continued to stand by the sliding doors. "I read

that insert you wrote this morning about Marla Tra-laine's unfortunate death."

"I'm not sure I should have written it, but I did."

"Very well written, but that doesn't come as any surprise considering your preeminence in the publishing business."

"That's very kind, but writing a summary of a real murder doesn't fall into my area of expertise."

"Still, impressive. Marla was going to make a couple of movies for me. Were you aware of that?"

"I recently became aware of it."

"It probably wouldn't have worked, even if she'd lived," he said matter-of-factly. "Most difficult woman I've ever encountered."

I said nothing.

Still standing in his pose by the doors, he said, "I understand that not only do you write good murder mysteries, you've ended up solving a few. Real ones, that is."

"That's true, Mr. Teller. Unfortunately, I ended up in a position to do that. It was certainly never my intention."

"Are you looking to solve Marla's murder?"

"What I'm looking to do is to enjoy this crossing on the *QE2*."

"But I hear you're doing some snooping around."

"I don't wish to debate semantics, Mr. Teller, but I don't consider myself to be someone who snoops."

He ignored my comment, continuing, "Have you received your faxes yet from New York?"

I was surprised that he knew about that, and I suppose my face reflected it. It brought forth from him a small, almost cruel smile.

I replied, "No, I haven't. But I expect them later this afternoon." I wasn't about to give him the satisfaction of asking how he knew.

"I understand you're pretty tight with the Scotland Yard inspector who'll be investigating her death."

I couldn't let that pass: "To whom are you referring?"

"What's his name?—Sutherland?"

I said nothing. It was obvious he was either receiving tips from someone in the ship's communications room, or had gathered information from the network of correspondents working in his far-flung news division.

"I have to admit, Mrs. Fletcher, that I sometimes stand in awe of women like you."

I raised an eyebrow. "Only women?" I asked.

"Especially women. I've been a fan of your books for a long time."

I doubted whether he'd personally read any of my novels. Somehow, he didn't strike me as someone who read much, aside from financial statements.

"Which one of them did you like most?" I asked.

"I liked them all."

I was right. He hadn't read any of them.

"You've been the subject of some recent meetings in my organization."

"Oh? Why?"

"I've been thinking of launching a series of two-hour made-for-television movies, the way the British do with their mystery series. Original dramas introduced each week by a host—or hostess. I'd like to create a series of such movies out of your novels."

"I—"

"And, of course, with Jessica Fletcher acting as the on-camera host."

"That's very flattering, Mr. Teller, but I'm afraid I'm not a television personality. I write alone. I'm not a performer."

"I understand your lecture yesterday was great."

"Thank you."

"I'm talking a significant deal here, Mrs. Fletcher. A lot of money. Having your books translated into TV movies would do wonders for sales."

"For sales? You mean for your advertising sales?"

Now he came to a chair across a small table from where I sat and took it. He narrowed his eyes as though that would help make what point he wanted to get across. "No," he said. "I'm talking about book sales. Nothing like steady television exposure to sell books."

"I wouldn't debate that with you," I said. "I've done my share of public appearances, including television, in order to sell a new book when it comes out. But frankly, Mr. Teller, my books sell extremely well. Each one is a bestseller."

"That may be so, Mrs. Fletcher—you don't mind if I call you Jessica"—It wasn't a question, simply a statement of what he intended to do—"I'm talking tripling, quadrupling your sales. Make you some real money."

I felt the hair stand up on the back of my neck. But I said calmly, "I'm quite comfortable with my life and professional career. Some of my books have been made into movies. I'm sure you're aware of them."

"Yeah, but I wasn't very impressed. We'll put enough money into them to make sure the production values are the best. Top casts. When I take on a project, I insist that it be the best. There's never any second best for me."

I'd had enough of his arrogance. I stood and said, "Perhaps you'd like to discuss this with my agent once you're back in the States. His name is Matt Miller. He's in New York and—"

"I don't deal with agents. I like to deal directly with the talent."

"I've enjoyed meeting you," I said, taking a few steps in the direction of the door. "Perhaps we'll see each other again before Southampton."

"That won't happen," he said. "Let me give you a word of advice."

I was tempted to say that I didn't need advice from him, but allowed him to continue.

"Forget about this Marla Tralaine incident. She was nothing but trouble. You don't strike me as somebody who wants or needs trouble."

"Am I to take that as a threat, Mr. Teller?"

"What I'm saying is that the smart way to get through life is to go for the things that make you rich, and avoid the things that don't. I'm offering you a sweet deal, Jessica. Focus on that and forget about Tralaine."

"Nice meeting you, Mr. Teller."

It took me ten minutes to calm down. By the time I had, it was almost time to go to the tea dance. Why did he want me to forget about Marla Tralaine and her murder? Had *he* murdered her, or had someone else do it at his behest?

I called the *QE2*'s communication center and inquired whether any faxes had come through for me. None had; I asked them to be on the lookout for any that might arrive and to let me know.

I tried again to reach George Sutherland in London. No luck. I placed a call to Seth Hazlitt in Cabot Cove, feeling a little guilty I hadn't tried earlier to return his call. No success there, either.

I looked at my watch. It was time to freshen up, change my clothes, and get to the Queens Room.

I was on my way out the door when the phone rang. I picked it up quickly, thinking it might be the communications center informing me that my faxes from Ruth Lazzara had arrived. Instead, it was the TV plant lady, Elaine Ananthous.

"I was just leaving, Elaine," I said. "Going to the tea dance. Will you be going?"

She started crying.

"Elaine, what's wrong?"

"He's missing."

"Who's missing?"

"Troy."

"Troy Radcliff?"

"Yes. I'm afraid something terrible has happened to him. He's gone."

"Calm down, Elaine," I said. "This is a huge ship. He's probably found a quiet corner in which to read a book."

"No, Jessica, I know something terrible has happened to him. I had the steward check his cabin. He didn't sleep there last night. No one has seen him anywhere on the ship today."

"Well, Elaine, if you're that convinced something has happened to him, I suggest you go to shipboard security."

"I was going to, but I'm so upset. Would you go with me?"

If anyone had been in my cabin with me, they would have seen the frustration written all over my face. All I wanted to do was go to the tea dance and bask in the wonderful music of the Tommy Dorsey orchestra. I'd gotten on the *QE2* to relax. It had been a long, hard winter. I'd written a play, read two others by friends, and had finished my latest book. I was tired, but ready for some fun.

"P-l-e-a-s-e," she said, crying again.

"All right," I said. "Meet me at the security office in ten minutes."

I knew one thing as I hung up on her. The offer Cunard had made me of another free crossing would not be forgotten.

Chapter Seventeen

Elaine Ananthous was at the security office when I arrived. She was her usual agitated self. Her eyes were red from crying, and her wispy, mouse-colored hair was in free flight. As I entered the office, she leaped from her chair and threw her arms about me. I managed to extricate myself and suggested we sit.

"Something terrible has happened to Troy," she said, voice quivering. "I just know it."

"When was the last time you saw him?" I asked.

"Last night. After dinner. He was with that dreadful man, Di Giovanni."

"Yes. I had a late dinner with them. They left the Queens Grill together. Where did you see them?"

"In the Golden Lion Pub."

The Golden Lion Pub was a *QE2* nightclub where rock 'n' roll music kept the dance floor filled into the wee hours. Somehow, I couldn't picture Elaine Ananthous frolicking there. Come to think of it, I couldn't picture Troy Radcliff gyrating to a rock beat, either.

"Did you have a drink with them?" I asked.

"No. I would have. With Troy. But not with Di Giovanni there."

I glanced at the closed door to Security Chief Prall's private office. "Does he know you're coming?" I asked.

"Yes. He told me he was busy, but would talk to me shortly."

"Elaine, why are you so convinced something bad has happened to Troy?"

"Because he wouldn't have . . ." She started crying again.

"He wouldn't have *what?*"

"He wouldn't have missed my lecture," she managed, her words choked.

Was this the only factor upon which she based her fear? I wondered. If Radcliff had seen her lecture before, his decision not to attend was understandable. An insensitive thought on my part.

I turned to her. "Surely, Elaine, missing your lecture isn't reason to—"

The door opened and Wally Prall came to us. "Sorry," he said. "This Tralaine business is dominating my every waking moment."

"Understandable," I said. "Mr. Prall, Ms. Ananthous believes something might have happened to her friend Troy Radcliff, the famous mountain climber."

"So she's said." He pulled up a chair. "Now, Ms. Ananthous, suppose you tell me why you think this is so."

She repeated that Radcliff hadn't attended her lecture that morning, adding, "I spoke with his steward. Troy didn't sleep in his bed last night."

"How can the steward be sure of that?" Prall asked.

Elaine shrugged, pulled a tissue from her purse, and blew her nose loudly.

"Perhaps we should talk to this steward," I offered.

Prall closed his eyes and sighed. I understood. He was swamped with responsibilities regarding the murder of Marla Tralaine and didn't need to launch a search for a passenger based upon what appeared to be irrational reasoning, a passenger who'd probably decided to hibernate out of public view.

He opened his eyes. "All right," he said. "I'll get the steward to come here. What's Radcliff's cabin number?"

Elaine gave it to him.

As she did, it suddenly struck me that Elaine's intense concern for Troy Radcliff could possibly stem from their having some sort of personal—intimate?—relationship. They made an unlikely couple, in my mind, but that meant nothing. I learned long ago never to judge why any two people are attracted to each other.

Prall disappeared into his office to summon the steward. I looked into Elaine's green, watery eyes and asked, "Is there another reason, Elaine, that you have this concern about Troy?"

"What do you mean?"

"I don't know. I just sense that there might be a . . . what shall I call it? . . . there might be a bond between

183

you and Troy Radcliff that goes beyond just . . . knowing each other."

It was as though I'd physically struck her. She stiffened, pressed her lank lips tightly together, and stared straight ahead.

"Elaine?"

I could barely hear her when she said, "Is it that obvious?"

"Then there *is* a certain . . . bond . . . between you and Mr. Radcliff?"

"It's too personal to talk about," she said, still in her rigid posture.

I wasn't about to press it. She was right; her personal life was none of my business.

Except, there was now the probability that her fear about Radcliff was based on more than his not having showed up to hear her lecture. Maybe I should take it more seriously, too, I decided.

Prall returned. "The steward is busy serving passengers in that section. Come on. We'll go to him."

He led us from his office to the hallway, off which Radcliff's cabin was situated. When we reached it, Elaine stepped back, as though afraid to enter. The steward came from the cabin across the hall and said hello to Prall.

"This is Mrs. Fletcher and Ms. Ananthous," Prall said.

"I know," said the steward, smiling slyly at Elaine.

"Did you tell Ms. Ananthous you didn't think Mr. Radcliff slept in his cabin last night?" Prall asked.

"Yes, sir. When she came looking for Mr. Radcliff, I brought her into his cabin. The bed was made just the way it was yesterday afternoon."

"And you've checked again?" Prall asked. "He's not there now?"

"I haven't gone back in," the steward replied.

"Let's take a look," Prall said.

The steward opened the door to Radcliff's cabin. I turned to Elaine to see whether she was following us inside. She wasn't. She remained pressed against the hall wall, fright written all over her face. I didn't press her to join us. Better she remain outside.

Radcliff's cabin was much like mine, although the color scheme was different. His built-in furniture was blond; mine was black. The layout was basically the same, except I noted he did not have a closet adjacent to the bathroom, as I did.

I observed that Troy Radcliff was a neat individual. There wasn't a thing out of place. His highly polished shoes were lined up with military precision in the closet. His clothing was hung so that the jackets faced in the same direction, and the space between them was equidistant. There was the faint aroma of male cologne in the air.

Prall went to the bed. It was made, as the steward said it had been, the bedspread pulled taut, not a wrinkle to be seen.

Prall asked the steward questions about when he'd last seen the cabin's occupant. As he did, I took the opportunity to peruse the bathroom. Like the main cabin, it, too, was a monument to neatness and order. Radcliff's toiletries were arranged in a cluster in a corner of the marble sinktop. Every label faced forward. His toothbrush stood at attention in a glass. A nail brush rested on the surface. The man was obviously pristine in his hygiene.

I rejoined Prall and the steward in the living room.

"Find anything?" I asked.

"No," Prall replied.

I went to the desk. On it were printed materials about the ship, along with the daily programs that had been delivered to the cabin. I opened the drawer and saw, among other things, a wallet. I called Prall over and pointed to it.

He picked the wallet up, turned it over in his hands, then opened it. I watched as he first examined the folded money section, withdrawing a wad of bills and counting it. There was a little over four hundred dollars. He next looked at the photos secured in clear plastic sleeves. There were six of them. Two were of Radcliff posing at the summit of unnamed mountains. There was a color snapshot of two dogs. Another depicted a small group of people at a celebration of some sort, laughing and looking happy.

The fifth photo was of actress Marla Tralaine. It appeared to have been taken years ago, at the height of her career. It had the look of posed celebrity photographs one finds in picture frames displayed for sale, or in empty wallets in a leather goods shop.

Prall and I looked at each other, our arched eyebrows reflecting what we were thinking.

He turned to the sixth picture. It was of the TV plant lady, Elaine Ananthous.

"That's her outside," Prall said.

"Ms. Ananthous. Yes."

He dropped the wallet on the desk, picked up the phone, and called his office to request one of his officers be sent to the cabin. I picked up the wallet and went through other items in it. A small slit created a pocket within. I wiggled my fingers into it, felt slips of paper, and pulled them out, unfolding each and reading. There were two.

The first contained small, meticulous writing with a fine-point pen. It said: "Dr. Jessup—final word—terminal—six months." There was a phone number added at the end of the cryptic writing.

The second slip of paper had a printed message on it, which I read with interest: "A dying man needs to die, as a sleepy man needs to sleep, and there comes a time when it is wrong, as well as useless, to resist." The name "Stewart Alsop" appeared in smaller letters.

I certainly recognized the name—Stewart Alsop, the famed journalist who'd succumbed to cancer a number of years ago.

"Mr. Prall," I said, handing him the notes.

He read them, looked at me, and said, "Sounds like Mr. Radcliff was a sick man."

"Seems that way."

We said it in unison: "Suicide?"

"I'll have a security force search the ship for any sign that Mr. Radcliff might have taken his life."

"Gone overboard?" I asked.

He nodded.

"It's happened before?"

"On rare occasions."

Prall's assistant arrived, and Prall issued the order to go over every area of the ship. "Quietly, of course," he added.

"I'd like to speak with Ms. Ananthous," I said.

"Think she might know something?" Prall asked.

"I think she probably does, considering how concerned she was that something bad had happened to Mr. Radcliff."

"Talk to her. She seems to trust you," Prall said. "I have to get back. Let me know if you learn anything."

"Of course."

Elaine had wandered to the end of the hall, where it joined another corridor leading to the nearest staircase.

"What did you find?" she asked when I reached her.

"Elaine," I said, "it's obvious you and Mr. Radcliff were very close."

"I really would rather not—"

"You don't have a choice," I said sternly. "Despite

his incredibly healthy appearance, he was a very sick man, wasn't he?"

She let out a whoosh of air, leaned against the wall, and focused on the floor.

"Look at me, Elaine," I said. "Troy Radcliff was dying. We found notes in his cabin."

"No," she said. "They said he was. But he was so strong. He was fighting it. I was helping him. He wouldn't die. He wouldn't allow that to happen to him. Happen to . . ."

"To *us?* You and him?"

"Yes."

"Did he ever talk to you about taking his life?" I asked with difficulty.

"He wouldn't do that."

I said nothing, my silence announcing clearly that I was waiting for a different answer.

"Yes," she said weakly.

"Since he's been on the *QE2?*"

"Yes."

"Weren't you worried that he would follow through?"

"No."

"If you'd taken him seriously, told others about it, he might have been dissuaded from taking his life."

"He has?" she asked, eyes opening wide. "Troy is dead?"

"I don't know. Mr. Prall and his security staff are going to thoroughly search the ship. We shouldn't jump to conclusions." I might have chosen a better descriptive term.

She slumped against the wall and wrapped her frail arms about herself. I was tempted to embrace her, but didn't. We stood together in silence. I assumed she dwelled upon the possibility that Radcliff had committed suicide. My thoughts were on the photo of Marla Tralaine found in Radcliff's wallet, along with Elaine's picture. I wanted to ask about it, but didn't feel it appropriate, at least as it applied to her. Whether George Sutherland would find it useful information when he took over the investigation was another matter.

"I'd like to go into his cabin," she said.

"Troy's? Why?"

"Just to be there . . . in case he calls."

"I don't think he'd call his own cabin, Elaine."

She pushed away from the wall and walked quickly down the hall. She seemed so fragile, so upset, that I felt it was incumbent upon me to stay with her. I checked my watch. It was four-thirty. The tea dance was half over.

Mr. Prall had left the door open to Radcliff's cabin. Elaine entered, and I followed. The events of the past few hours had diverted my attention from the *QE2*'s motion. It hadn't seemed to have become more pronounced. I looked across the cabin to the porthole, through which a setting sun tossed a stream of yellow light across the carpet.

Elaine stood in the middle of the room and looked

around. My eyes went to the desk. Prall hadn't taken Radcliff's wallet with him, nor had he bothered to put it back in the drawer. I took a step in that direction, but Elaine was quicker. She scooped up the wallet, raised it close to her face, and opened it. I waited for her reaction to seeing Marla Tralaine's picture nestled in there with her own. When she did, she gasped, and dropped the wallet to the floor. I wasn't sure what to do, so I did nothing until she slowly went to the bed, flung herself on it, and began to sob.

I picked up the wallet and put it in the desk drawer. "Elaine," I said softly.

She continued to cry.

"Elaine," I repeated, perching on the edge of the bed and placing my hand on her arm. "Please. Tell me about it."

She sat up, leaned forward, and placed her hands on her knees, her posture that of total defeat. I took a tissue from a box on the nightstand and handed it to her. She removed her glasses, dabbed at her eyes, and dropped the limp tissue to her lap. She turned and looked into my eyes.

"Elaine?" I said.

"I might as well," she said.

Chapter Eighteen

By the time I walked Elaine Ananthous to her cabin, the tea dance I wanted so much to attend was over. But I decided to head to the Queens Room anyway to see whether I could catch up with the gentleman host, Sydney Worrell, the aging British actor who'd appeared in *Dangerous Woman* with Marla Tralaine.

Although the Dorsey Band had finished playing, the room was still filled with happy, toe-tapping passengers. I stood at the edge of the dance floor and took in faces at the tables. Mr. Worrell sat with four unattached women. They were having a spirited, upbeat conversation, and I decided not to intrude. The eight gentlemen hosts on the *QE2* were expected to continue their conversational and dancing services right into the evening hours to women traveling alone, including being on tap as dancing partners to the beat of the ship's orchestra in the Grand Lounge. I'd seek him out there later. If I felt the situation was right, I'd bring up to him what I'd learned about his past association with Marla Tralaine.

As I stood there, it occurred to me that my shipboard friend, Mary Alice Ward, was at that moment being served a gourmet Italian meal prepared by the famous television chef, Carlo Di Giovanni. That struck me as something I'd enjoy watching, and went to the Grand Lounge where my murder mystery play—I considered it "mine" because I'd written it, although it certainly belonged to Rip Nestor and his Malibu Mysteries—was performed each afternoon.

The crowd gathered to watch the cooking demonstration was large, almost as many people as had attended the play that afternoon. Di Giovanni was up on the stage. The ship had provided an elaborate cooking set for him, including ample counter space, a stove and oven, and myriad pots, pans, and utensils. A wireless microphone was attached to the front of his white chef's jacket. He wore a classic high, puffy chef's hat.

The demonstration had already started when I arrived. I didn't bother looking for a seat, content to lean against a pillar from which I had a clear view of the stage.

To Di Giovanni's immediate right was an immaculately set table at which Mary Ward sat. The table was covered with a white linen tablecloth; crystal and silver sparkled in the glow of the stage lights. Mary had dressed for the occasion, looking lovely in a stylish powder blue suit and white blouse with a fluffy collar. She sat prim and proper in her chair, hands folded on the table, her usual inquisitive, slightly bemused expression on her face as she watched Di Giovanni prepare the meal, his nonstop commentary explaining every step as he sliced and stirred and cooked. I gathered that the menu consisted, at least in part, of an endive salad spiced with special ingredients he claimed only he uses, an appetizer of braised mushrooms with a garlic-tarragon sauce, a version of veal piccata from a recipe he announced had been in his family for four generations, and a rice dish.

He was very entertaining, each move done with great flourish, and his running dialogue—I had the feeling he embellished his Italian accent for such demonstrations and when appearing on TV—was witty and charming. No pun intended, he had the audience eating out of his hand.

He'd just made an elaborate presentation of the salad to Mary when a voice behind me said, "Mrs. Fletcher."

I turned. It was my onboard hostess, Priscilla Warren.

"Yes, Priscilla?" I asked.

"These just arrived for you."

She handed me a sheaf of faxes.

"Splendid," I said.

"Enjoying the cooking demonstration?" she asked.

"What? Oh, yes, very much, although I think I'd better read these right away."

I could have put off going through the faxes in order to see the rest of the cooking demonstration, but the one on top of the pile was too compelling. It was a photocopy of the front page of the tabloid newspaper Mary Ward had remembered, and told me about following her run of good luck in the casino. She'd said she believed that the aging actor in the play, Ron Ryan, was the man depicted on that front page as Marla Tralaine's lover at the time of the murder of the actress's husband.

I went to a vacant club chair in the wide hallway and spread the faxes on the table in front of me. I took a moment to glance out the large window. The day's welcome burst of sunshine had given way to a hazy gray. Was the storm that had supposedly changed course, and that was now bearing down on us, about to become a reality? No sense worrying about it, I knew. Among many things over which I had no control, the weather topped the list, especially on the notoriously fickle North Atlantic.

I started reading.

Although the tabloid front page had been reduced in size, and was at least two generations removed from the original, there was no doubt in my mind that Mary was right. The man pictured was a younger Ron Ryan. The caption beneath his photograph identified him as Don Bryan, allegedly one of Marla Tralaine's lovers. Don Bryan? I thought. He certainly hadn't been very original in choosing a new name.

I put that fax aside and started going through the

others. Ruth Lazzara had done a splendid job, as she always does. A good researcher knows precisely where to go in search of information. As far as I'm concerned, she's the best in the business.

She'd included a long article from the Los Angeles *Times* that provided a detailed recap of the murder of Marla Tralaine's husband and subsequent investigation of it. The prosecutor was quoted at length. As far as he was concerned, sufficient evidence had been gathered to go to a grand jury for an indictment against the slain man's wife, the famed actress Marla Tralaine.

Her attorney was also quoted. He dismissed the prosecutor's claim as "pure political rubbish," adding that when the investigation of the murder was completed, it would be obvious to all that instead of being a murderess, Marla Tralaine was a grieving widow. He further stated that in his opinion, the murder had to do with Marla's husband's reputed links to Las Vegas gamblers and mobsters.

The article was accompanied by three photographs.

One was of Tralaine, dressed in black and holding a handkerchief to her face. The caption read: "A tearful Marla Tralaine attending the coroner's inquest into her husband's murder."

The second photograph was of her dead husband. It had been taken a few years earlier in Las Vegas, and showed him with a group of men. They all held cigars and had their glasses raised in a toast to something celebratory. Behind them was an unnamed Las Vegas casino.

The third picture was of the crime scene. In it a young man I assumed was a police forensic expert, wearing a white lab coat, was on his hands and knees, his fingers touching the carpet where Tralaine's husband's body had been found. Even though it was a black-and-white photo, the bloodstain on the carpet was obvious.

There were two other people in the photograph, identified only as LAPD detectives.

I put that fax aside and went on to the next. But then I went back to the LA *Times* story and examined it more closely, straining to see faces better in that third photo. After studying it for a minute, I sat back and again looked out the window.

Could it be?

I looked at it again.

"Yes," I said to myself softly. One of the detectives in the picture looked very much like the actor playing the role of my detective in the play, Billy Bravo.

Jerry Lackman.

Mary Ward said she thought his accent pegged him as a Californian, not a New Yorker, and I'd agreed with her that afternoon while watching him perform. Also, he said he had heard about Tralaine's murder through "official channels."

Was he an actor playing a police officer?

Or was he a real police officer?

I went on to the next fax. Ruth Lazzara had done a remarkable job of digging up material on everyone I asked about. The one I now read was from the New York *Times* business section. It detailed the growth of the Teller Cable Network, presenting a not terribly flattering picture of Sam Teller. The writer did point out, however, that Teller's business acumen was highly respected in the broadcasting industry.

Most of the piece was a dry analysis of how he'd built his empire from a single station in Charlotte, North Carolina, into a giant rivaling the other large networks. I wasn't quite sure why Ruth had included this article until I reached the end of it. Teller, according to the *Times* writer, was poised to enter the motion picture business in a big way, using his network as a showcase for films to be produced under the Teller banner. His plan of action, the article said, was to avoid high-priced current motion picture stars, featuring instead actors and actresses of yesteryear who'd fallen out of the public limelight, but whose names were still well known to millions of Americans, particularly older ones. Teller's philosophy ran counter to the prevailing television marketing theory that all shows and movies must be shaped to appeal to a younger audience.

In an interview he'd granted for the article, Teller pointed out that America was, indeed, "graying," and that these were the people in our society who had the discretionary income to spend on advertiser products. In that sense, I was squarely in Samuel Teller's corner.

His first two films would star Marla Tralaine, although it was pointed out that negotiations between Tralaine's manager and the Teller Network had been difficult, bordering on combative.

Ruth had also faxed me profiles of current popular personalities on the Teller Network, including its on-air chef, Carlo Di Giovanni, adventurer Troy Radcliff, Judge Dan Solon, and the plant lady, Elaine Ananthous. They didn't provide me with anything of particular interest.

The next piece of paper was one of those having-lunch-with-a-celebrity pieces that appear from time to time in newspapers. This was a sit-down with Marla Tralaine. The picture of her was a fairly recent one; the writer who interviewed her pointed out that the setting had been carefully chosen by Marla and her people. They lunched at a secluded corner table where the restaurant's lighting was augmented by special lights brought in by Tralaine's manager to create a more youthful glow.

The interviewer was good. She started with a series of softball questions that allowed her subject to give easy, flattering answers about herself. But as the interview progressed, the questions became harder, more personal and probing, eventually trespassing into Marla Tralaine's private life.

When asked about her multiple marriages, she replied that each man she'd married had been good in the beginning, but quickly showed his true colors. The interviewer asked what specifically she meant by that. Marla replied, "Simply that they quickly proved they did not match up to my expectations of a husband."

The interviewer retreated to a few gentler questions before returning to the subject of the actress's personal life.

"You have children," the interviewer said.

"Yes."

"Are you close to them?"

Here the writer indicated that Tralaine paused for a very long time before answering. When she did, she said, "As close as I wish to be."

"And how close is that?"

"I see them now and then. Jasmine—she's my daughter—lives in Europe. We touch base whenever I'm there."

"You have a son, don't you?" the interviewer asked.

"Yes. I'd like more tea."

"Is he in show business, too?"

"He's . . . Rip is . . . ah, the waiter. More tea, please."

I dropped the fax to the table. "Rip?" The only Rip I knew was Rip Nestor, director of the murder mystery play I'd written.

I picked up the page and continued reading. Tralaine

finished her response to that question with, "He's doing quite well."

"He's in show business?"

"I'd like another cup of tea," was her response.

As I continued reading the material sent me from New York, laughter from the Grand Lounge reached my ears. Evidently, Di Giovanni's presentation was going over well, and I imagined Mary Ward enjoying her specially prepared meal at the hands of this master chef.

One of many reasons I looked forward to this five-day crossing on the QE2 was that I viewed it as five days of simplifying my life. Nothing to do but have a good night's sleep, choose food from the lavish menu three times a day, listen to some music, take walks on the deck, and read a good book cover to cover.

It had ended up anything but that. In concentrating on the faxes, I'd forgotten about the events of an hour ago, the disappearance, and possible suicide, of famed mountain climber and TV adventurer, Troy Radcliff.

The sounds from the Grand Lounge made me want to return there to enjoy the demonstration—toss the faxes overboard. I'd missed that day's tea dance. People I'd met were not who they seemed to be.

I tried to renew my focus on the papers before me, but the sounds coming from the lounge were too magnetic. I arranged the faxes in a neat pile, tucked them under my arm, and returned to my previous position from where I could watch the conclusion of the presentation.

Di Giovanni had served Mary the appetizer of mushrooms in his special sauce and returned to the mock kitchen to apply the finishing touches to his veal.

I watched Mary Ward at the table, a broad smile on her face, and seeming not the least bit uncomfortable being in front of a large crowd.

Di Giovanni turned to her from where he stood at the stove and asked, "The truth now. Aren't they the best mushrooms you have ever tasted?"

A microphone had been set up next to her. She leaned closer to it and said, "Oh, yes, they certainly are. But I don't eat mushrooms, so I don't have any way of comparing your dish to—"

Stopping in midsentence caught my attention; I tensed to better see and hear what was happening.

Mary pulled back from the microphone, her smile replaced by a frown. Her hands went to her stomach. Her eyes opened wide—a pained groan was picked up by the mike and broadcast throughout the Grand Lounge.

Di Giovanni was so immersed in his cooking he was oblivious to what was happening. The rest of the audience hadn't caught it either, at least not initially. But when Mary slumped down in her chair, her fingers still pressed tightly against her stomach, and more anguished sounds came from her, it became evident to all that something was terribly wrong.

"Oh, my God," I said, circumventing the tables and heading for the stage. Di Giovanni was now aware, too, although the realization had frozen him into inaction.

Priscilla Warren, who'd been backstage, quickly came to Mary's side and said into the microphone, "Is there a doctor in the house?" Then, she shouted, "Get someone from Medical up here right away."

"She looks like she's been poisoned!" a woman yelled from the audience.

"Mushrooms!" someone else shouted. "It must have been the mushrooms."

Di Giovanni started talking into his microphone, his hands waving wildly. "No, it's not the mushrooms," he said, his voice booming through the speakers.

People from the audience crowded in front of the stage.

I jumped up onto it and knelt next to Mary, who was obviously in pain. "Help is coming," I said, hoping to comfort her.

"I don't want to die," she said, her voice weak.

"Don't be silly," I said, stroking her arm. "You'll be fine."

A number of QE2 staff milled about on the stage, waiting for medical help to arrive. I looked up at them from my position low to the floor. As I did, I saw her, only a fleeting glance as she quickly left the backstage area and disappeared from view.

What was Elaine Ananthous doing there?

When I'd left her in her cabin, she'd seemed completely drained, incapable of doing anything but resting on the bed.

But here she was, backstage at a cooking presentation by a man she despised.

She'd given a lecture on using poison to kill people.

Simplify my life during five days on the QE2?

What a quaint, misguided concept.

Chapter Nineteen

I waited until Mary Ward was carried away on a stretcher by two uniformed ship hospital workers before stepping down from the stage.

"Where are you going?" Priscilla Warren asked.

"Back to my cabin. I have calls to make, and some thinking to do."

"I'll go to the hospital and make sure everything is being done for Mrs. Ward."

"Thank you," I said. "She's a remarkable woman. I only met her a few days ago, but I feel as though we've been friends for years."

"I understand."

"I'll check in on her, too."

I passed through the casino on my way to the stairs to One Deck, where my cabin was located. Dozens of passengers were already pulling slot machine handles and betting on the turn of the roulette wheel. I'd stopped for a moment to observe the action when Security Chief Prall approached.

"Yes?" I said.

"I just heard about Mrs. Ward."

"She's quite ill. It happened so suddenly."

"Food poisoning," he said. "Mushrooms, I understand, prepared by that TV chef."

"No one knows that for certain. At least not yet."

"This is becoming an unpleasant crossing," he said.

"Events have certainly taken the edge off its pleasantness," I said.

"And I'm determined to see that nothing else happens before we reach Southampton."

"I hope you're successful."

"I've met with my staff and other ship's officers. We've tried to establish a pattern that we can use to head off other incidents."

"A pattern?"

"Identifying those passengers who might be at special risk."

"I'm not sure I follow."

"Ms. Tralaine was accompanied on the ship by three people—her manager, Mr. Kunz, her physical fitness coach, Mr. Silvestrie, and her hairdresser, Ms. Malone."

"And?"

"We feel they need special security for the duration of the crossing."

"Who else have you identified?"

"You, for one, Mrs. Fletcher."

"Why me?"

"Ms. Tralaine was also aboard as a lecturer. It could be that her killer is targeting lecturers."

"I'm not sure I follow that logic, Mr. Prall. Ms. Tralaine is the only lecturer to have been 'targeted,' as you put it. Mrs. Ward isn't one."

"But she was taking part in a lecture."

He was right, of course. Still, I didn't think that event supported his thesis.

"And there's the disappearance of Mr. Radcliff."

"You're right," I said. "Anything new on the search?"

"Not yet. Mrs. Fletcher, I've ordered that each person I've named—Ms. Tralaine's people and all remaining lecturers—be assigned a security guard until we reach Southampton."

"I suppose that's prudent, although I hope it doesn't become intrusive. Despite what's happened, there's still three more days to enjoy, which, by the way, I intend to do."

"Good point, Mrs. Fletcher. I'll see to it that everything is kept low-key."

"There are others who might fit this pattern you've established."

"Oh? Who?"

"Mr. and Mrs. Teller."

"Why them?"

"Mr. Teller was involved in nasty negotiations with Ms. Tralaine's people over two movies he wanted to star her in."

"I wasn't aware of that," he said. "But there's really

no danger to them. They're spending the crossing secluded in their penthouse."

"Next to Ms. Tralaine's penthouse."

"Yes, but—"

"And it isn't as though they're without visitors. I've visited Mr. Teller at his invitation. Mr. Kunz evidently spends considerable time there working on new projects without Ms. Tralaine—now that she's dead. And one of the actors in my play has been there."

"Your point is?"

"My point is that it's highly unlikely that Ms. Tralaine was murdered by a stranger. It was someone she knew, possibly from the very list of people you've developed. There's no telling how many of them have been invited to Mr. Teller's penthouse. All the lecturers, with the exception of me and Ms. Tralaine, work for him on his cable network. I've been told there's intense infighting among these people over whose show stays on the air and who goes."

He listened intently, a frown creating deep creases in his wide forehead. "Hmmmm," he muttered. "You're saying I should expand my number of people we protect."

"No, I'm not necessarily suggesting that, Mr. Prall. What I *am* saying is that there are more people on this crossing with links to Ms. Tralaine than you're aware of."

"I see."

Should I tell him that one of his gentleman hosts had appeared in an old Marla Tralaine film? I decided to.

"How thoroughly are the backgrounds of your gentleman hosts checked?" I asked.

"Why do you ask that?"

"Well, it's just that one of them, a Mr. Sydney Worrell, once acted with Ms. Tralaine in a film, *Dangerous Woman*."

"Yes, I know."

"You do?"

"To answer your first question, Mrs. Fletcher, every employee on the QE2 has undergone a thorough background check. It's management philosophy that our passengers deserve to be served only by top-notch men and women. That extends to every level."

"I wouldn't expect less."

"Sydney included his acting career on his résumé when he applied to become a gentleman host. He mentioned he'd made a movie with Ms. Tralaine."

"What was his reaction to her death?"

"He was asked about that. He said he knew her only from making that one picture. In fact, I understand he tried to make contact with her just to say hello after she boarded. He sent up a note to her penthouse. She ignored it."

"Are you sure she never responded to his note?"

"That's what he told people. He laughed about it, I understand."

"Will you excuse me?" I said. "I need to make some calls from my cabin."

"Of course. I've assigned someone to you. He should be waiting."

"I really don't think that's . . . all right. Thank you, Mr. Prall."

Sandy, the junior officer who'd escorted me to my cabin when I boarded, was in the hall outside my cabin. "Evening, Mrs. Fletcher," he said.

"Good evening, Sandy. Are you here to be my security guard?"

He smiled. "Afraid so."

"I didn't realize you were in the security department."

"I'm not, but they're running a little shorthanded and thought I might be up to the job."

"I'm sure you are. I'd invite you in, but I have private calls to make."

"Of course. I'm not to intrude on your privacy. I'll wait right out here."

I closed the door behind me, sat on the bed, and picked up the phone. Rip Nestor answered on the first ring.

"Hello, Rip," I said. "It's Jessica."

"Oh, hi. What's up?"

"I wondered if we could get together tonight. Perhaps right after dinner."

"Sure. But why? Something wrong?"

"No. I just need to run something by you."

"Okay. Where?"

"The Chart Room?"

He laughed. "I didn't take you for a bar type," he said.

I let the comment pass.

"What time?" he asked.

"Nine?"

"I'll be there. By the way, how did you think the show went this afternoon?"

"I thought it went quite well."

"Glad you liked it."

"Rip."

"Yeah?"

"I'm fascinated with two of your cast members—Jerry Lackman and Ron Ryan."

"Why?"

"No special reason. I've had a chance to speak with both and find them interesting. Do you know a great deal about them?"

"Sure. I mean, I know their acting credentials."

"I'd love to see their résumés. Do you have them with you?"

"No. They're back in California."

"Just thought I'd ask."

"Sure it's just idle interest?"

"Of course. What else would it be?"

"I don't know."

"Well, have to make other calls. See you at nine."

"Yeah. Nine."

I tried another call to Seth Hazlitt in Cabot Cove. This time I was successful.

"Jessica? Are you calling from the ship?"

"Yes."

"Sounds like you're next door."

"Modern technology at work. How are things back there?"

"Everything's 'bout the same as when you left. Only been a couple of days, Jessica. Not time for things to change. I understand that's not the case with you, however."

"You heard about Marla Tralaine?"

"Of course I did. Saw it on the TV show with that James Brady fella. He mentioned you."

"I know. I was there during his broadcast."

"Hardly what you expected on your . . . crossin', is it?"

"Yes. And no, it's not what I expected. You tried me before, Seth. I'm returning your call."

"*Ayuh.* I called—so did Mort—just to ask how things were goin' on the ship, and to say we arranged with the caterin' folks to deliver a bottle 'a the best Champagne to your table."

"That's sweet, Seth."

"They do that?"

"Not yet, but I'm sure they will. Probably tonight at dinner."

"You make sure they do, Jessica. Cost a pretty penny."

"I'm sure it did."

"But now that I know the actress, Tralaine, has been murdered right there on the ship with you, I'd like to know what you're doin' about it."

" 'Doing about it'? What do you mean?"

"Protectin' yourself is what I mean. You've got yourself a murderer loose on board. No tellin' who he'll go after next."

"I'm not worried, Seth. The ship's security staff is top-notch. I have a personal security guard standing outside my cabin door as we speak."

"Well, I'm pleased to hear that. How's the weather?"

"Good. It was sunny most of the day, but it's clouded up now. We might run into a storm."

I was sorry I'd said it.

"Not a proper place to be in a storm, Jessica. The North Atlantic has taken its share of big ships."

"I think the storm has veered away from us, Seth. I have to run. Love to Mort. No need for me to return his call, is there? You'll tell him what we talked about."

"*Ayuh.* I'll tell him we spoke. Drivin' me crazy, with all his talk about the play he gave you."

"Have to run, Seth. Love to all. See you in about a week."

I called George Sutherland's London office and was pleased he was there. But he sounded angry.

"Something wrong, George?" I asked.

"The local press has been calling, asking about the

plan to helicopter to the ship to investigate Ms. Tralaine's murder."

U-h oh, I thought.

"I may be wrong, Jess, but I can't remember telling
anyone on the *QE2* of that plan but you. And, of
course, the security people."

I kept my voice light. "Oh, you know, George, how
things like that are bound to get around."

"The story was filed by a reporter on the ship with
you. Name is . . . ah, yes, Hamish Monroe."

"I've met him. He wanted to interview me. I put
him off."

"Good decision, I'd say. Prudent to avoid the press
at all costs. He mentioned a woman named Ward as
the person who discovered the body."

"She . . . I'll fill you in on that when you arrive. Any
idea when you'll be flying in?"

He hesitated. Was he reluctant to give me more
details about the question?

But he answered my question. "Day after tomorrow,
weather permitting. I checked with our meteorologist
an hour ago. You might be facing a nasty storm in the
next twenty-four hours."

"I'd heard something about that," I said. "Really
bad?"

"Could be. Well, Jess, it's good hearing from you.
Mother Nature cooperating, I'll see you soon. On the
QE2."

"I look forward to it. Thanks, George."

"For what?"

"For . . . being you."

Concluding our conversation was sad. But I sensed George was under the gun, and I had things to do, too, beginning with a trip to the ship's hospital to check on Mary Ward's condition.

Sandy was waiting patiently when I left my cabin.

"Are you going to be with me everywhere I go?" I asked, heading for the stairs.

"Afraid so, Mrs. Fletcher. Where are we going?"

"The hospital. My friend took ill during the cooking demonstration in the Grand Lounge."

"Sorry to hear it."

"She's an older woman," I said, modifying it with, "a little older than I am. Food poisoning can be especially hard on an older person."

"Food poisoning?"

We rounded the corner and headed down the midships staircase to the Two Deck, near the G Stairway where the hospital and Dr. Russell Walker, the *QE2*'s medical director, were located.

"It looked that way," I said over my shoulder.

"From our food?"

I stopped walking and turned to him. "Cunard prides itself on its food, doesn't it?"

"Oh, yes, it certainly does."

"Unlikely, isn't it, that ingredients provided by the ship to the TV chef for his demonstration would be tainted?"

"Very unlikely, Mrs. Fletcher. Unless he brought his own food aboard."

"Yes, that's a possibility."

But not probable, I thought.

I paused at the door to the medical suite. I was almost afraid to step inside. Despite my optimistic prognosis for Mary Ward, I harbored a parallel fear that she might be deathly sick.

I couldn't shake seeing Elaine Ananthous at the cooking demonstration. I'd conjured a scenario over the past hour. There was no reason for Elaine to attempt to poison someone like Mary Ward. But it was possible, considering her fragile personality, hatred of Carlo Di Giovanni, and fear of losing her television show to his Italian florist friend, that she could be irrationally driven to do something to ruin Di Giovanni's cooking demonstration. If that scenario proved accurate, my new friend, Mary, just happened to be in the wrong place at the wrong time.

"Going in?" Sandy asked.

"Yes."

I wasn't prepared for what I saw. Seated in a blue vinyl armchair in the reception room was Mary Alice Ward. Aside from being pale, she didn't look any the worse for wear after her experience.

"Hello, Jessica," she said.

I sat next to her. "Mary. How are you?"

"A little shaken, but otherwise pretty good. Healthy southern stock, I suppose."

"I was so worried. Last time I saw you you were . . . well, frankly, you were green, and in pain."

"My stomach still hurts a little, but not too bad. It happened so fast. I was enjoying myself until I picked at those two mushrooms."

"It was good there were only two, and that all you did was pick."

"I don't really like mushrooms, but didn't want to be a spoilsport for Mr. Di Giovanni. All I know is that all of a sudden I had these terrible cramps. And then, almost as fast, they were gone."

"Thank God for that," I said, exhaling. "What did the doctor do for you?"

"He examined me and gave me some medicine."

"And he says you're okay now?"

"Yes. I said I just wanted to sit here a spell before going back to my cabin."

"Where is Dr. Walker?" I asked.

"Visiting a sick passenger in his cabin." She looked up at Sandy, who stood in the doorway.

"He's my bodyguard," I said.

"Bodyguard? My goodness. I wonder . . ."

"What, Mary?"

"I wonder if I could speak privately with you, Jessica." She glanced at Sandy again.

"Would you mind?" I asked him.

"Sure."

When he was gone, she leaned closer to me and whispered, "Ms. Tralaine was strangled."

217

I sat back hard against the chair, got over my shock, and said, "Would you repeat that?"

She said, "Ms. Tralaine was strangled."

"How do you know?" I asked, lowering my voice to match hers.

"I looked."

"Mary—"

"I didn't look at the body, although I would if I could have. I peeked in the morgue. The room is off that other room over there." She pointed.

"And you went in there?"

"Just poked my head in."

"So how do you know she was strangled?"

"There was a report lying on a cabinet just inside the door—an autopsy report. I don't think they do a complete autopsy, but they obviously examined her."

"Why do you say that?"

"Because it said under 'Cause of Death' . . . no, it said 'Apparent Cause of Death' . . . that the cause was strangulation. I saw some notes about bruises on her throat. I would have read more, but I heard someone coming and didn't want to be caught."

"I—"

"I hope you aren't angry with me for taking a look. I just thought that as long as I was down here anyway, I might as well."

I stood. "Feeling well enough to walk with me to your cabin?" I asked.

She stood, too. "Oh, yes," she said. "I'm feeling much better."

"Know what?" I asked.

"What?"

"I'm feeling much better, too. Come on, Dr. Watson. We have some more talking to do."

Chapter Twenty

I spent a half hour with Mary Ward in her cabin.

She'd developed a theory of who killed Marla Tralaine, and laid it out for me with clarity and precision. Although it was only that—a theory—it made a great deal of sense, particularly her speculation on why Marla was naked when dumped into the lifeboat on the Boat Deck. I understood why my newfound North Carolina friend had won the murder mystery contest in her hometown. Her deductive powers were as impressive as her physical resilience.

During our conversation, I offered everything I'd learned about those aboard the *QE2* who'd had some connection with the slain actress, as well as those who were involved in pursuits that might provide a motivation for murder.

I showed her the faxes I'd received from Ruth Lazzara, including the long interview with Marla Tralaine in which she'd let slip—that's the way I read it—that she had a son named Rip.

"Your director's name is Rip," Mary said.

"Exactly."

"Which might explain why his copy of the script, the one with all his notes and comments, was found in her penthouse."

"It could explain it," I said. "This crossing might have been viewed as an opportunity for them to reestablish their relationship."

"But you said that when you had lunch with him in New York, he used an unflattering term to describe her."

"Which wouldn't be surprising, considering the apparent estrangement between them. At least that's what I got from reading the interview with her."

"Do we know who the father is?" Mary asked.

"No. Any ideas?"

"Well, let me see," she said. "There's the actor, Mr. Ryan, who we now know was romantically involved with Ms. Tralaine at the time of her husband's murder."

"Right."

"And there's that gentleman host we danced with. He was in a movie with her."

"But that's no secret, according to the ship's security director. He put it on his résumé when he applied for the job. And she didn't respond to the note he'd sent her, wanting to say hello."

"According to him."

"According to him."

"I've been wondering about that physical fitness trainer," she said.

"Mr. Silvestrie?"

"Yes. Strange, at least to me, that he was with Mr. Teller's actress wife, Ms. Sims, up on the promenade. Remember?"

"He pushed away a young autograph seeker."

"Why would *he* be so protective of her? After all, Jessica, he worked for Ms. Tralaine. Not for Ms. Sims."

I nodded. "Worth thinking about," I said.

"You say Mr. Kunz . . . is that his name?"

"Marla Tralaine's manager."

"You say he's been meeting with Mr. Teller about other projects for Mr. Teller's network?"

"That's what he told me."

"Certainly is fast, wouldn't you say?"

"Fast in the sense that it's terribly soon after his boss's murder?"

"Exactly. Poor dear isn't even cold in the ship morgue, and he's discussing new business deals. Almost makes you wonder whether he's happy she's no longer around."

"Perhaps he is—happy. What other thoughts have you had, Mary?"

She smiled, went to the porthole, and looked out over the dark, churning North Atlantic. "It's getting rough," she said.

"The sea."

"And the people."

She turned to me. "Do you know what I'm in the mood for?"

"What?"

"A lavish dinner in the Queens Grill."

I laughed. "You can't be serious, considering what you've been through."

"Oh, but I am serious. I'm one of those people who's always believed in getting back on the horse once you've fallen off."

"It's formal tonight," I said.

"Then I can wear a special outfit I brought with me just for the occasion. My daughter, Katherine, bought it for me especially for this trip. She's a lawyer in New York, although she's now decided to become an English teacher."

"Good for her. And I look forward to seeing what she bought for you."

"I'll show it off at dinner."

"Oh, Mary, by the way, I've arranged to meet Rip Nestor tonight at nine in the Chart Room."

"Yes?"

"I intend to be direct with him about whether he's Marla Tralaine's son."

"Sometimes being direct is the best policy. See you at dinner in, say, an hour?"

"Sounds good to me."

"I just hope one thing."

"Which is?"

"I just hope they aren't serving mushrooms tonight. If they are, just seeing it on the menu could set me back."

* * *

I went to my cabin and chose a dress my Cabot Cove female friends and I had decided upon during my impromptu modeling session prior to the trip. It was the fanciest item in my wardrobe, a floor-length sequined emerald green number that was an inch away from being too tight. Mary's upbeat attitude had buoyed my spirits, too, although any ebullience was tempered by the disappearance of Troy Radcliff. I assumed, perhaps foolishly so, that the security office would call me the moment they came up with information about him. I tried to stop thinking about what might have happened to Radcliff, especially the worst-case scenario—that he'd taken his life by leaping into the sea because of a terminal medical prognosis.

Thoughts of him naturally kept Elaine Ananthous in mind, too. She'd confessed tearfully to me after we'd returned to her cabin that she and Radcliff had, indeed, been more than professional colleagues. It hadn't been a torrid romance. They'd entered into what she termed a "caring relationship" based upon mutual respect.

"He thought I was funny," she'd said. "Nobody else thinks I'm funny. Strange, maybe. Funny because of the way I look and talk. Laughing *at* me, not with me. But he always laughed *because* of me."

That she spoke of him in the past tense was not lost on me.

I felt increasingly sad for her as we talked, woman to woman, especially when she got into her physical relationship with Radcliff. Not that she described it in graphic terms. I would have been surprised if she had. She said that Troy Radcliff not only looked remarkably young for a man his age, his hormones had reflected it, too.

She spoke of his many affairs with beautiful women, including Marla Tralaine.

"What brought them together?" I asked. "She didn't strike me as a woman who'd enjoy climbing mountains."

"Sam Teller introduced them. At some party, I think. It didn't mean anything to Troy. None of his affairs did. That's why he needed me in his life. I was always there for him, no matter what."

Carrying Tralaine's photo in his wallet gave credence to what Elaine Ananthous told me. Unless, of course, Troy Radcliff was nothing more than a fawning fan with an overactive imagination. I seriously doubted that was the case.

I had left Elaine's cabin with a heavy heart. My shipboard experiences with her had not been especially pleasant, or uplifting. She was, to use a phrase, a strange bird, dreadfully unsure of herself, suspecting the worst in people, paranoid, and even vindictive.

But she was also a vulnerable creature, a woman who'd forged a special career for herself despite obvious shortcomings, and who looked for love and affection—a human being.

As I applied the finishing touches to my makeup, my sympathetic feelings for her were tainted by what I believed to be true—that she'd tampered with Carlo Di

Giovanni's mushrooms in order to injure his reputation. That an innocent person—in this case, Mary Ward—had suffered as a result, made it that much more upsetting. Of course, I couldn't prove Elaine had done it. But it was one of those instinctive moments we all experience now and then, when we just know we're right.

"Where the hell is everybody?" Judge Dan Solon growled after I'd joined him at our table. Mary Ward had arrived moments before; there were only the three of us.

"They must have had other commitments," I said, glancing at Mary. Her daughter's choice of a dress had been a good one. It was a simple, yet elegant beige sheath that complemented her perfectly, especially now that she'd regained color in her cheeks and sparkle in her eyes.

"I understand you had a bout of food poisoning," Solon said to Mary.

"Yes."

"Happened during the chef's demonstration?"

"Yes, although I don't blame—"

"I wouldn't eat anything that madman cooks," he said, handing down an irrefutable sentence.

Jacques, our waiter, announced the evening's specials that weren't listed on the menu. "For a beginning," he said, "we have mushrooms prepared in a savory butter-garlic sauce that is—" He pressed his fingertips to his lips and blew a kiss to the table. "That is—"

"Why don't we just get to the entrees?" I suggested, looking to Mary, who managed a smile.

Across the room, James Brady shared a table with the other journalists on board, including the British reporter, Hamish Monroe, and the stars of the previous night's musical entertainment, Pamela Fiori and Michael Cannon from *Town and Country*. They were in high spirits, judging from the laughter and unending flow of Champagne.

In fact, the entire dining room was festive that particular evening. It certainly wasn't the weather. The seas had become increasingly rough throughout the day. Was the storm getting closer? Hopefully, it wouldn't keep George Sutherland and his people from flying to the ship on our fourth day at sea, one day out from Southampton.

We enjoyed our dinner, although the other lecturers were missed. Judge Solon didn't know that Radcliff had disappeared, and that a search was under way. Di Giovanni had told the judge right after the incident with Mary that he was having dinner in his cabin for the duration of the crossing. As for Elaine Ananthous, I would have been surprised if she'd shown for dinner.

Despite the gaiety surrounding our table, we had relatively little to say to each other. Mary's gastronomical experience hadn't diminished her appetite, judging by the vigor with which she ate. We were on dessert when the maitre d' came to the table and handed me a note. I opened it, read, stood, and said, "Excuse me, please."

Mary's expression asked whether she should come with me.

"I'll be back in a minute," I said.

Security Chief Prall stood just outside the dining room. "Sorry to interfere with your dinner, Mrs. Fletcher."

"That's quite all right. I was almost finished."

"We've come up with something on Mr. Radcliff's disappearance."

"Oh?"

"This."

He removed a shoe from a bag and showed it to me.

"His?" I asked.

"Evidently, although that hasn't been confirmed. I thought maybe Ms. Ananthous might be helpful."

"There's just the one?"

"Yes. We found it on the Two Deck Aft."

"Near the rear of the ship. The stern."

"Exactly."

"And you found just this single shoe?"

"That's right."

I examined the shoe again. It was highly polished, just as all of Radcliff's shoes had been when I saw them in his cabin. It also appeared to be of a style that was consistent with his other footwear.

"Any idea why only one shoe was found?" I asked.

"No."

But I had one. If Troy Radcliff had committed suicide—leaped into the sea—he would have done it with both shoes on, or both shoes off. That only one was found said to me that if he *had* gone over the side into the North Atlantic, it was not a voluntary act.

"Have you spoken with Ms. Ananthous about it?" I asked.

"Not yet. You seemed to have forged a relationship with her. I thought it might be wise to have you with me when I ask her about the shoe."

"I'd really rather—"

"Only take a moment. I called her cabin. She's there, and I asked her to stay."

"All right," I said. "Let me tell my table companions I won't be back for coffee."

When I returned to the table, I leaned close to Mary's ear and said, "There may be news about Mr. Radcliff's disappearance. Will you wait for me, let's say, in the lounge outside?"

"I'll be there."

"What's the rush?" Solon asked.

"No rush," I said. "Just a personal matter."

"Going to the casino?" he asked Mary as I started walking away. "Could use some of your good luck."

"I don't think so," she replied. "My gambling days are over."

I followed Prall to Elaine's cabin. She took a long time responding to Prall's knocking. When she did, seeing me seemed to unnerve her. "What are you doing here?" she asked.

"Mr. Prall thought I might be helpful, that's all," I replied. "If you'd rather I—"

Prall resolved the question by gently ushering me into the cabin with a hand on the small of my back.

"Ms. Ananthous, we found this on one of the decks," Prall said, removing the shoe from the bag and holding it out for her.

"Troy's shoe," Elaine said.

"You're sure?" Prall asked.

"Yes. Where did you find it?"

Prall told her.

"Where's the other shoe?" she asked.

"We don't know," Prall said.

Elaine slowly sat on the bed, wrapped her thin arms about herself, and began rocking. Prall looked at me and raised his eyebrows. I nodded. It was best to leave her alone.

As we went to the door, Elaine asked, "How is that older woman?"

I stopped and turned. "Mary Ward?"

"Yes."

"She's all right. Fortunately, she had only a taste of the mushrooms, if that's what actually caused her poisoning."

"I didn't mean to hurt her."

"Would you excuse us?" I asked Prall.

His quizzical expression said he wasn't sure what was transpiring.

"Please," I said.

"I'll be outside."

I joined her on the bed. "You did it to embarrass Mr. Di Giovanni, didn't you, Elaine?"

"It was so stupid of me. I snapped, I guess. Lost my head."

"You never stopped to think of killing Mrs. Ward?"

My question spurred renewed animation. "Oh, no, that was never a problem. I put such a small amount of poison on the mushrooms that even if she ate all of them, she'd only become ill."

" 'Only become ill,' " I said, unable to keep disdain from my voice. "It was a terrible thing to do."

"I thought everyone would think it was his mushrooms that made her sick. But I can't live with that lie. I can't live with myself." She started to cry and went back to her rocking motion.

I got up and went to the door, looked back, then suffered a wave of pity and left.

"I gather that had to do with the woman getting sick at the cooking lecture," Prall said.

"Yes. But it's been resolved. Anything else I can do for you before I rejoin my friends?"

"As a matter of fact, there is."

I drew a deep breath and exhaled.

"There's a videotape I'd like you to see."

"Of what?"

"Of Two Deck Aft."

"Where Radcliff's shoe was found?"

"Yes. Can we keep what I tell you between us?"

"That depends."

"Mrs. Fletcher, we've had a couple of suicides from Two Deck Aft over the years."

"Oh?"

"It's . . . it *was* a spot where going over the side was somewhat easier than other locations on the ship."

"I see."

"We took steps to correct that situation, including installing a hidden surveillance camera."

My heart skipped a beat. Was he about to announce they'd taped Troy Radcliff's demise?

"Because you've been so involved with this unfortunate incident from the beginning and have cooperated with us, I'd like you to be among those invited to view this tape."

"Well, I . . . yes, of course. Where is it?"

"In our communications center. It's just one segment of hundreds of hours of tape from Two Deck Aft. They're working on it now, trying to narrow it down to cover only the period during which Mr. Radcliff might have been there. There's also the problem of picture quality. It varies, depending upon the weather, and how well the equipment is working."

"When do you think you'll have it ready?" I asked.

"I don't know. As soon as possible, of course. I'll let you know."

"All right. I appreciate being included."

"Frankly, Mrs. Fletcher, I'm well aware you've been busy looking into Ms. Tralaine's murder ever since you and Mrs. Ward discovered her body. Maybe by watching the tape, you'll be able to put to better use what you've already discovered."

"Are you suggesting her murder and Mr. Radcliff's disappearance are linked?"

He gave me a wan smile. "Mrs. Fletcher," he said, "I leave that entirely up to you. Go back to your friends. I'll let you know the minute the tape is ready for viewing."

Finding out there was a videotape that might possibly shed light on what happened to Troy Radcliff was exhilarating. At least one mystery would be solved before we reached England. No, there would be two mysteries solved, now that I knew for certain that Elaine Ananthous had, indeed, put something on Carlo Di Giovanni's mushrooms.

I headed straight back to the Queens Grill Lounge where Mary Ward waited. She sat with James Brady and the British journalist, Hamish Monroe. I wasn't sure I liked her being with them. She knew everything I knew, with the exception of what I'd just learned about the shoe, the tape, and Elaine's confirmation that she'd tampered with the mushrooms.

"Jessica," Brady said, getting up and pulling a chair closer, "off investigating?"

"No," I said, continuing to stand. "What would I be investigating?"

"The whereabouts of that aging mountain goat, Troy Radcliff."

"You do get around, Mr. Brady."

"My calling, Jess. Well? Where is he?"

"I don't know," I said, truthfully, but barely so.

He gave me that smile that has elicited information from a who's who of the celebrity world. "Have no idea, Jess?"

I said to Mary Ward, "You and I have someplace we have to be."

She raised her eyebrows, realized I was attempting to extricate us from the situation, and said, "That's right, Jessica. I almost forgot."

"Before you go," Hamish Monroe said, "a question?"

"Yes?"

"I hear The Yard is flying in to investigate Marla Tralaine's murder."

"It is?"

A mischievous laugh from Brady. "Come on, Jessica, you know it's true."

Mary and I stood.

"And a rather good chum of yours is in charge," Monroe added. "Sutherland?"

"No comment," I said.

We started to walk away, but Mary stopped, turned, and said firmly, "And there'll be no comment from me, either."

Chapter Twenty-one

"Where are we going?" Mary asked.

"We're not going anywhere. We're leaving."

"Because they're members of the press."

"Exactly."

Sandy, the junior officer assigned to me, had waited outside the Queens Grill during dinner. He fell in behind us at a respectful distance.

We strolled with no particular destination in mind, passed the movie theater, and ended up at the Grand Lounge, where stagehands prepared for the evening's entertainment. The ship's movement had become more pronounced; I noticed that even Mary, who'd been so surefooted, was having trouble navigating the undulating floor.

"Aren't you supposed to meet your director, Mr. Nestor?" she asked.

"Oh, that's right." I checked my watch. "I'd forgotten. It's nine."

"You'd better go."

"Care to join me?"

"I don't think that's wise," she said, "not if you intend to ask him directly whether he's Ms. Tralaine's son."

"I'm not sure I will, Mary. After all, I'm basing my suspicion purely on something she said a few years ago during a newspaper interview."

"Sometimes little things like that tell great tales."

I looked at her and smiled. "You're right," I said. "I'll ask him. But I don't think having you there would be inhibiting."

"I'd just as soon not," she said. "I haven't done any shopping yet, and promised to bring things back for my children and grandchildren. You know, small souvenirs of the trip."

"All right. I'll meet up with you later. Say an hour?"

"Right here?"

"Right here."

I went down one level to the Quarter Deck, with Sandy at my heels.

"Where are you off to next?" he asked.

"I have to meet the director of my play—in the Chart Room. I'd appreciate it if you could . . . well, Sandy, make yourself inconspicuous while I'm with him."

"No problem. I see a friend. I'll be outside at one of the window tables."

"Thanks for understanding."

When I entered the elegant Chart Room, Rip Nestor was already seated at a table for two.

"Sorry I'm late," I said.

"It's okay."

I took the remaining vacant chair.

"Crowded tonight," I said.

"Like a big party all over the ship."

"Spirits are high, despite the weather."

"Supposed to get worse overnight," he said.

"The handrails will get a workout."

A pretty young waitress took my order of a white wine spritzer. Nestor had a dark ale in front of him. When my drink was served, I raised my glass. "Here's to a successful production."

He touched the rim of my glass with his heavy mug. "So, what's on your mind?" he asked, sipping.

"Well, Rip, I've been busy since Marla Tralaine's body was discovered."

"Yeah?"

"I was asked to get involved by the ship's security director, Mr. Prall."

"That's pretty obvious, Jessica. The announcement in the daily program and all."

"No. Beyond that. I've taken it upon myself to try and find out who killed—"

His smile was crooked. "Find out who killed Marla?"

"Yes. Was she . . . were *you* close to her?"

It was a forced guffaw. "Close to her? What do you mean?"

I sighed, then closed my eyes, opened them, looked directly at him, and asked, "Are you Marla Tralaine's son?"

I didn't know what his reaction would be. He might have angrily denied it, refused to acknowledge it, stormed from the room, or . . . or, perhaps, admit it was true. I waited and watched.

He sat back in his chair and took another drink of his ale. I couldn't read what he was thinking, contemplating, intending to say or do.

"Why do you think I might be?" he asked into the glass mug, eyes focused on its contents.

"I read an interview with her done a few years ago. The interviewer asked about her children. She mentioned a daughter, Jasmine, living in Europe. When she was asked about a son, she said 'Rip,' and went on to another subject. The only Rip I know is you . . . Rip."

"And that's why you think I'm Marla's son?"

"That, and . . . when we had lunch in New York, I mentioned her. You called her a 'bitch.' "

"So?"

"I took from that that you knew her."

"No, it doesn't necessarily mean that. She has that reputation."

I said nothing.

"Doesn't she? Have that reputation?"

"I suppose so. But since we've been sitting here, you've referred to her twice as 'Marla.' "

"I—"

"That says to me you knew her better than just having met her on this ship."

He finished his ale and motioned for the waitress to bring another.

"I think I'm right," I said.

He glared at me, looked away, chewed on the knuckle of his right index finger, and ignored the fresh mug of ale set before him. That he'd ordered a second drink was promising. If he intended to leave, he wouldn't have bothered.

"I don't know why you would deny it, Rip. Being the son of a famous movie actress isn't something to be ashamed of."

He quickly reestablished eye contact with me. "I'm not ashamed."

I slowly exhaled. He'd admitted it.

"Why does it matter to you whether I'm Marla's son?"

"It doesn't. And it does."

He looked confused.

"From a personal perspective, Rip, I have no interest in whether Ms. Tralaine was your mother, and what your relationship was with her. But she's been murdered. On this lovely ship. It's my instinct that being her son could—and I stress *could*—have something to do with why she was killed, and who killed her."

239

He sat up straighter. "You aren't suggesting that *I* might have killed her, are you?"

"No. But I've been putting together a number of disparate pieces since her death. Maybe you can help me make better sense of them."

He drank. So did I.

I waited what I considered to be an appropriate amount of time before pressing further. "Rip, is your father on board?"

"Him? What do you care about him?"

I decided I might as well share as much of what I knew as necessary to keep him talking.

"Was your father the man who was murdered while married to your mother?"

His chin sank to his breastbone, and he slowly shook his head.

"Your mother had a lover when that husband was killed. He's on this crossing. His name is Ron Ryan, although that wasn't his name when he was involved with her. Then he called himself Don Bryan."

"Jesus."

"You know that, don't you?"

"How did you find *that* out?"

I thought of Mary Ward. She'd been the one who'd remembered Ryan-Bryan's picture in the tabloid newspaper. "With a little help from a friend," I said. "Did you know who he was when you booked him to play Morris McClusky in the play?"

I didn't need an answer because I was certain that had been the case.

He confirmed it.

"You said he pleaded with you for the part."

"Yeah. He was down and out. He's gambled away every cent he's ever made."

"I have the impression you don't pay your actors very much. I'm not being critical of you, Rip. The point I'm making is that in pleading for the part, Mr. Ryan wasn't about to improve his financial picture, especially with a casino on board."

"Meaning?"

"I just wonder whether he wanted to be on this ship, on this particular crossing, because he knew she'd be on it, too."

"To kill her?"

I shrugged.

"Ron's not capable of killing anybody."

I reserved judgment and decided to keep going, as long as he was willing to be open with me.

"Do you know one of the ship's gentleman hosts, a Sydney Worrell?"

"No."

"He's British. He was in a film with your mother. *Dangerous Woman*."

"Don't know him."

"Okay. I've been told that the mountain climber, Troy Radcliff, had an affair with your mother."

He downed the rest of his ale and waved for

another. "Big deal," he said to me. "She had affairs with the world."

"That's pretty harsh."

"But true. She was married four times. Lovers? I can't count that high."

"Anyone I know?" I asked.

"I don't know."

"I mean, anyone on this ship?"

The waitress brought his third mug of ale. He pushed it away, pulled out his gold Cunard credit card, and handed it to her.

"I have the feeling our little meeting is over," I said.

"I have to be someplace."

"You don't have to buy."

"My turn. You picked up lunch in New York."

"All right. Rip, can I say one final thing?"

"Why not? You seem to have a lot to say."

"I want to get to the bottom of who killed your mother. If you know anything else that might help, I'd appreciate hearing it."

"Sure."

The waitress brought the receipt. He signed it, then stood.

"Jerry Lackman," I said matter-of-factly.

"Huh?"

"Jerry Lackman—playing Billy Bravo."

"What about him?"

"You told me you knew only of your actors' and actresses' acting credentials."

"Right."

"But you knew about Ron Ryan's personal background."

"So?"

"I just thought you might know about Jerry Lackman's personal life, too—his life *before* he became an actor."

"Good night, Jessica. This has been a lot of fun. Do me a favor."

"If I can."

"Forget about Marla being my mother. I don't need the rest of the ship, let alone the world, knowing it."

I felt sorry for him as he walked from the Chart Room and joined the flow of passengers in the broad hallway. The children of famous celebrities so often were scarred by their parents' public lifestyle and private indiscretions. I was pleased, of course, that I'd confirmed my suspicions that he was the son of Marla Tralaine. But that was only a self-serving satisfaction with little value beyond me.

What I needed to do was to put it into context, one that would help solve Marla Tralaine's murder. What had started as an innocent involvement on my part had now taken on a sense of urgency. It had become an obsession of sorts, one that had overtaken me, and would drive me for the duration of the crossing.

Chapter Twenty-two

Mary Ward and I arrived at the Grand Lounge at the same time, coming from different directions. She carried two large shopping bags.

"Successful shopping spree," I said as we found an empty table. Sandy, my security guard, stood with another junior officer a few feet away.

The dance floor was filled with happy passengers moving to the orchestra's infectious beat. A musical revue would come later, featuring a group of young singers and dancers who, according to other passengers, were immensely talented. I hoped to see them perform before reaching Southampton.

"I bought out the store," Mary said.

"So I see."

"I have four children to buy for. And there are all the grandchildren."

"Keeps you busy."

"And young, I think. How did your meeting with the director go, Jessica?"

I told her what had transpired.

"You were right," she said.

"I was lucky, seeing that interview with Marla Tralaine. Without the fax, I wouldn't have known anything about Rip Nestor possibly being her son."

"How does it fit into the bigger picture?" she asked.

"I thought you and I could talk about that."

"You know I'd enjoy that."

"There's more," I said.

"Oh?"

I told her about Troy Radcliff's shoe being found on Two Deck Aft, that a search for him was under way, and that a recently installed security camera might have captured on tape what happened to Radcliff, assuming he went overboard from Two Deck Aft. After some internal debate I also told Mary that Elaine Ananthous had admitted she'd tainted the mushrooms that made her ill. To that, she said, "She must be a desperate, sad woman to have done something like that."

I had a few other descriptive terms to apply to Elaine, but decided they were too harsh to be expressed.

"Well, Jessica, you said you wanted to talk this out with me. Do we start now?"

I looked around the Grand Lounge. "No, not here. Too public. Besides, there are other people I'd like to speak with before we try and put it together."

"Later, then?"

"Yes."

"I'll go back to my cabin and do some thinking alone. I love doing crossword puzzles, Jessica, and this is like a puzzle, only it involves real people."

"And murder," I added.

"And murder."

"Give me a few hours," I said. "I'll come by your cabin."

I stayed at the table after she left and watched the dancers, soaking up the moment of relative, albeit brief peace. I thought of how wonderful a North Atlantic crossing on the *QE2* was, the vacation trip of a lifetime, memories to last forever.

Provided, of course, you weren't diverted by murder.

I was about to leave when a deep, cultured voice from behind said, "Care to dance, Mrs. Fletcher?" I turned and looked up at Sydney Worrell, the gentleman host who'd appeared in *Dangerous Woman* with Marla Tralaine.

"Why, yes," I said. "I'd enjoy that."

The band played "Moonlight in Vermont" as Mr. Worrell led me to the floor. We said nothing to each other for the first few bars of the song. Then he said, "I understand you've been asking about my relationship with Marla Tralaine."

"Mr. Prall told you?"

"No. Someone else. Marla and I were in a movie together."

"Dangerous Woman. I've seen it."

"Enjoy it?" he asked, expertly turning me in another direction.

"Yes. You played the butler."

"Just another version of a gentleman host."

"I understand you tried to communicate with her after she boarded."

"Yes, quite. Sent up a note to her penthouse. Never heard from her. No surprise."

"Why did you want to see her?" I asked.

The band segued into "Moonglow," at the same tempo.

"Just to say hello for old time's sake. Wasn't even sure she'd remember me. Maybe she didn't."

"So you never got to see her before she died?"

"Afraid not. You know, Mrs. Fletcher, the butler isn't always guilty, although in your popular fiction you might see it another way."

I laughed. "I've never had a butler do it in any of my books."

"That's good news. Good news, indeed. I hear The Yard will be flying in soon, unless this bloody storm that's approaching dashes that plan."

"You've heard about that plan?"

"Oh, yes. I also hear—we have an active grapevine on the ship—that you're actively involved in trying to determine who killed Marla."

"I'm interested," I said, allowing him to dip me.

"Any suspects?"

"No."

"Not what I hear."

"Oh. Tell me what you've heard."

The song ended, and the band launched into something with a rock 'n' roll beat.

"Not my style," I said.

He escorted me back to the table. "May I?" he asked, indicating an empty chair.

"Of course, although I'll be staying only a few minutes."

Sitting across from him gave me the opportunity to observe him more closely. He was one of those men who aged gracefully, like Troy Radcliff, although Worrell was not the physical specimen Radcliff was. He had a face that I was certain maintained its ruddy glow at all times. Because he was fair, small blemishes on his face and liver spots on the backs of his head were more pronounced than on people with darker skin.

"You dance nicely," he said.

"You lead nicely."

"I won't keep you," he said. "But might I be so bold as to offer an opinion?"

"You already have—about my dancing."

"I was thinking of murder."

"Then by all means give me an opinion."

"Do you know that one of the actors in your play was once Marla's lover?"

"Ron Ryan."

He placed his hand over his heart and sighed. "You're obviously way ahead of me."

"Do you personally know Mr. Ryan?"

"I *knew* him, back when Marla's husband was killed."

"Knew him well?"

"Well enough to know what a bloody scoundrel he was. And is."

"Are you suggesting he might have killed her?"

"Decidedly not beneath him."

"I thought you knew Ms. Tralaine only because of the part you had in her movie. What caused you to know Ron Ryan so well?"

"He owed me money. We hung about together in Hollywood, looking for a break, wanting to become stars. Doesn't happen to most people, certainly not to me or Ryan."

"Did you know Mr. Ryan wanted very much to be in the acting troupe for this crossing?"

"No."

"Did you know he'd be on the ship?"

"No. Was surprised to see him. At the craps table, of course."

"Well, Mr. Worrell, thank you for the opinions, and for the dance."

We stood; he bowed slightly from the waist.

"Oh, one thing," I said.

"Yes?"

"Did you know that Marla Tralaine was booked on this trip when you applied for the job of gentleman host?"

"No, I . . . it wouldn't have mattered to me, I . . ."

I sensed he was lying. "Enjoy the rest of your evening," I said, walking away.

I decided to look for Jerry Lackman, the actor playing Detective Billy Bravo in my play. Of all the questions floating about in my overactive brain, he posed the most provocative one.

From what I'd seen in the faxes sent me by Ruth Lazzara, he'd been a young Los Angeles detective, part of the team investigating the murder of Marla Tralaine's husband. Now he was an actor. Nothing especially puzzling about that; other cops have turned to acting after their careers in law enforcement end.

But Lackman was appearing in a play aboard the *QE2* on the same crossing as Marla Tralaine. He claimed he was a native New Yorker, but his accent— and his career as a member of the LAPD—rendered that claim a lie.

Why would he lie about something like that? The only reasonable explanation I could come up with was that he wanted to hide the fact that he'd investigated Marla Tralaine's husband's murder.

That raised an even bigger *why?*

Was he *still* investigating that murder? If so, it wouldn't be in an official capacity. He was an ex-cop.

It then occurred to me that if sticking with that case was his reason for being aboard, it could be in the role of a private investigator, a PI. Pure speculation on my part, but a possibility. If so, who'd hired him? Private investigators don't work for nothing.

I knew where I'd find Ron Ryan and Judge Solon—at the craps table.

Where would Lackman choose to spend his evening on the ship? Working out in the spa? Becoming computer literate in the Computer Learning Center? Learning to square dance?

None of the above.

I didn't have to wonder for long. He came from the direction of the casino, walking with Marla Tralaine's personal trainer, Tony Silvestrie, and her manager, Peter Kunz.

I stepped back into a shadow so they wouldn't see me. They passed.

"Mrs. Fletcher," Sandy said, having broken away from his friend and joining me once again.

"Yes?"

"On our way again?"

"Yes. I feel like a walk."

"I have to walk with you."

"I know."

"Anywhere special?"

"No."

I fell in behind Lackman and the others, staying far enough behind in the event one of them turned. They climbed the midships stairs to the next level, the Boat Deck, and headed for the Queens Grill Lounge. Sandy didn't seem to be aware that I was following them.

They went past the door to the lounge. Once it had closed behind them, I moved closer so that I could look through the glass. They went immediately to the door leading up to the penthouses, opened it, and disappeared behind it.

There were only two people up there they might be visiting.

One was Marla Tralaine.

But she was dead.

The other was cable TV mogul Sam Teller.

I bet on the latter.

As the saying goes, it was a no-brainer.

I turned to Sandy. "I think I'll make it an early night," I said.

"Yes, ma'am."

"Maybe have a cup of tea with my friend Mary Ward."

I said good night to Sandy outside my cabin, went inside, shut the door behind me, and looked out the porthole. The North Atlantic was angry that night, and becoming more so.

I stepped to the desk, where the computer provided by the Computer Learning Center for me to write the announcement of Marla Tralaine's murder still sat. They hadn't bothered to remove it.

I picked up the phone. Mary Ward answered on the first ring.

"Feel like a cup of tea?" I asked.

"That would be nice."

"I have an idea I'd like to discuss with you."

"Good. I have a few I'd like to discuss with you, too."

"Well, come on over, Mary. I think we have an interesting night ahead of us."

Chapter Twenty-three

Walter, our steward, delivered tea and cookies to my cabin.

"Mrs. Ward and I will be working late tonight," I told him. "We may need more room service later."

"Just call," he said. "Any time."

We sat in matching club chairs beneath the porthole.

"Where do we start?" she asked.

"You agree with what I want to do?" I said.

"Oh, yes. But do you think they'll go along with it?"

"We'll see. The first thing is for me to make that call to Ms. Jenkins."

Rose Jenkins, who put out the daily activity program, answered my call in her tiny office. "Yes, Mrs. Fletcher?"

"I have an important, last-minute announcement to go in the program," I said.

"I'm just about to print tomorrow's edition," she said.

"I understand. But you could include an insert, the

way you did with the announcement of Ms. Tralaine's death."

"What's the announcement?"

"A special one-act play to be performed tomorrow, right after Act Three of the murder mystery."

"A special play? What's it about?"

"It's about ... it's hard to explain. You'll better understand when you read the announcement."

"I'll have to clear it with the social director."

"That's fine, but give me a half hour before you do that."

"Sure."

"I'll deliver the disk to you within the hour."

I hung up, stood, and said to Mary, "I have a few people to see. I'll be back as soon as possible."

"Want me to go with you?"

"No. You stay here and keep jotting down your thoughts."

Sandy sat in a straight-back chair just down the hall. He jumped to his feet when he saw me appear.

"I need to see the cruise and social directors right away," I said. "Help me find them?"

"Sure." He picked up a wall phone and dialed a number, then asked that the two directors be paged. A few minutes later, I stood with them in front of the historic display in the Midships Lobby.

I explained to them what I intended to do. When I was finished, they looked at each other for reaction.

"Well?" I said.

"Fine with us, Mrs. Fletcher," the cruise director said. "But this involves Security."

"I'll talk with Mr. Prall," I said.

"Fair enough."

Mary sat at my desk, making notes, when I returned to the cabin.

"How did it go?" she asked.

"Fine."

I called Prall's office. He wasn't there, but was due back shortly. He called five minutes later.

"How are things progressing with the videotape?" I asked.

"Good. We've identified the section that covers the time period when Mr. Radcliff was on Two Deck Aft."

"When can I see it?"

He conferred with someone in his office. "A half hour?"

"That's good," I said. "Your office?"

"Yes."

"There's something else I need to discuss with you, Mr. Prall."

"Go ahead."

I told him of having met with the cruise and social directors, and outlined what I intended to do. He listened patiently. When I was through, he said, "That could be risky, Mrs. Fletcher."

"Not as risky as having someone else killed before we reach Southampton," I said.

There was a long pause on the other end of the line.

Finally, he said, "All right. We'll go over it when you get here."

"Will you call the others and tell them you approve?"

"I'll do it right now."

I pulled up a chair next to Mary at the desk.

"Sounds as though you're making progress," she said.

"Things are working out. Now, I'd better get this announcement written and down to Ms. Jenkins so she can print it and insert it in the program."

It took me only fifteen minutes to write it. Satisfied with the words on the screen, I stored the document on a fresh disk and went to the hallway.

"A favor?" I said to Sandy.

"Of course."

"Would you run this computer disk down to Rose Jenkins for me? She's expecting it."

"I'm not supposed to leave."

"You aren't intending to spend the entire night out here, are you?"

"No. Security is supposed to send someone to relieve me in an hour."

"All right," I said. "I'll deliver it myself."

"No," Sandy said. "I'll do it. You go in your cabin and lock the door. I'll let you know when I'm back."

I flopped in one of the club chairs and directed a stream of air at an errant lock of hair that had fallen over my forehead.

"I feel as though I'm not doing anything to help," Mary said.

"But you're about to begin," I said. "Ready to collaborate on a play with me?"

"I'm not a writer," she said.

"That may be true, Mary, but you are a thinker. Between us, I think we'll do just fine."

I came to the desk and inserted a fresh disk into the computer.

"But do you think Mr. Nestor will let you do it?" she asked.

"I think he wouldn't dare refuse. Now, let's go over the scenario you've come up with."

We discussed the plot for the one-act play for the next twenty minutes.

"I have to get down to the security director's office," I said.

"To see the tape."

"Yes. We'll start writing as soon as I get back."

The section of relevant tape ran only three minutes. I watched it four times.

"Shocking, isn't it?" Prall said after he'd stopped the VCR and turned up the lights.

"Yes."

"Sure you want to use it tomorrow?"

"Absolutely sure," I said.

"I've cleared it with our top people in London. They've agreed only because Scotland Yard is due to fly in at about the same time you'll be presenting it. Otherwise—"

"I understand," I said. "Now, I'd better get back. By the way, Mr. Prall, I was skeptical of your decision to provide security for the lecturers and those involved with Ms. Tralaine. I'm sorry I was. I think if anything, you'd better beef it up."

"I already have, Mrs. Fletcher."

"Well?" Mary asked when I came back to my cabin.

"You were right, Mary," I said. "Absolutely right. Now, let's get it down on paper."

Chapter Twenty-four

Early in my writing career, I occasionally wrote far into the night when faced with a crushing deadline. Even back then, it went against my metabolic clock. I am, and have always been, an early-to-bed, early-to-rise person.

But this night, with the *QE2* surging through the swells and waves of the North Atlantic on the way to Southampton, England, I'd never felt more awake and energetic.

Mary Ward and I worked side by side until three that morning. When we were finished, I removed the disk from the computer, held it up to her, and said, "I think that does it."

"I hope so," she said, covering a yawn with her hand.

"Sorry to keep you up so late."

"I wouldn't have missed it."

"Why don't you get to bed? We had a date to walk on the Boat Deck. I think we'd better skip it this morning."

"I still might do it," she said.

"But the weather."

"I'll see how it is four hours from now. Good night, Jessica."

"Good night, Mary. Thanks."

"It was my pleasure. But you do understand that the plot comes only from my imagination."

"I'd say it comes from more than that. Your ideas on why Marla Tralaine was murdered, and who might have done it, make a lot of sense to me."

"But what if I'm wrong?"

"We'll have stayed up late for nothing. No one will have been hurt. We're not using real names. On the other hand—"

"Yes. On the other hand."

After she was gone, I opened my door and peeked into the hallway, where a uniformed security officer sat in the chair.

"Excuse me," I said.

"Yes, Mrs. Fletcher?"

"I need to take this disk to the Computer Learning Center to have something printed from it."

"They're closed now."

"Yes, of course they are. Thank you."

I retreated inside and had Priscilla Warren paged. She answered her phone in a thick, sleepy voice.

"I know it's an ungodly hour to call, Priscilla, but I really need to have a computer printout from a disk before breakfast."

"Sounds important. What is it?"

"A play."

"A play?"

"You'll read about it in this morning's activity schedule. Can you arrange it?"

"Yes."

"Oh, and I'll need a dozen photocopies."

"Not a problem. I'll send someone to your cabin to pick up the disk, and have everything delivered to you by, say, eight?"

"Great. Thanks so much."

Fatigue now overwhelmed me. I dressed for bed, turned out the light, and closed my eyes. I assume I fell asleep right away because the next thing I knew, the daily activity program was slipped beneath the door.

I got up, but fell back on the bed. The ship was really reacting to its stormy environment.

Using the wall to steady myself, I picked up the program and made it to one of the club chairs. There it was, my brief announcement inserted into the main program.

ART IMITATING LIFE

Everyone on this magnificent ship was stunned to learn that one of its celebrity passengers, the actress Marla Tralaine, was found slain in a lifeboat on the Boat Deck.

Speculation has naturally been rampant since that grim discovery.

The events surrounding her murder have prompted me to write a one-act play, using what little we know of the murder as a basis for its story.

The play is a work of fiction. Whether you, the audience, finds a rational parallel to the real murder will be for you to decide.

This original play in one act will be performed today in the Grand Lounge, immediately following Act Three of the ongoing murder mystery play. Roles will be acted by the actors and actresses from that same play.

Jessica Fletcher

The phone rang.

"Hello?"

"Jessica? It's Rip."

"Good morning, Rip."

"What's this I'm reading in the program?"

"About the play?"

"Yes, about the play. What play?"

"One I just wrote. I was up half the night."

"Using *my* actors?"

"I didn't think you'd mind. It would just be a reading, not a production. I don't expect them to learn lines."

"I sure as hell do mind, Jessica. Hey, does this have to do with what we talked about last night?"

"There's a . . . there's an element of that, although it's more an aside."

"Well, forget it."

"You might want to reconsider, Rip."

"Why?"

"Because there are things about you and your relationship with your mother—and father—you might not want broadcast."

"That sounds like blackmail."

"It may sound that way, Rip, but I don't mean it to. How about getting together for breakfast? I can better explain in person."

"I still don't understand. From what I read, it sounds like you're going to solve Marla's murder on-stage."

"If only it were that easy. Breakfast? Seven?"

"Yeah. Okay. But I don't like this."

"You'll feel better about it after we get together. The Pavilion? Meet you at the door?"

"Yeah."

Although I'd had only an hour or two of sleep, I was bustling with energy. Showering wasn't easy because of the ship's motion, but I managed. I was in the cabin, drying my hair when the phone rang again.

"Hello?"

"Mrs. Fletcher?"

"Yes."

"This is Sam Teller."

"Good morning, Mr. Teller."

"I read about this one-act play you've written."

"I hope you'll be there to enjoy it."

"Why did you write it?"

"I'm not sure I'm obligated to answer that. But I will. This crossing has been a wonderful experience. I wanted to give something back to Cunard. You know, an extra added attraction."

"I'm not in the mood for jokes."

"I wasn't joking. Why are you calling me?"

"I'd like to see the script."

"Of the play? Don't be absurd."

"Maybe it'd make a good TV movie."

"Come watch and decide if it would."

"Maybe I will."

"I'd be honored. I have to run. Thanks for calling."

I hung up and felt a surge of excitement. I'd hoped the announcement of the play would generate some interest on the part of those associated with Marla Tralaine. That was my intention. But I hadn't thought that Sam Teller himself would call.

Or that I'd receive three other calls before heading for my seven o'clock breakfast date with Nestor.

"This is Peter Kunz, Mrs. Fletcher—Marla Tralaine's manager."

"Yes, Mr. Kunz. Up early, I see."

"I read about the play you're putting on this afternoon."

"I hope you'll be in the audience."

"You bet I will. I'd like to see the script."

"Why? It's meant to be performed, not read."

"Are you free for breakfast, Mrs. Fletcher?"

"No."

"I'd like to talk to you before you put on this play."

"I'm listening."

"No. In person, face-to-face. It might be worth your while to hear what I have to say."

"Would it have to do with Mr. Teller?" I asked.

"As a matter of fact, it would. He asked me to call you on his behalf."

"I've already spoken with him this morning."

"I know. When can we meet?"

"Nine? The Queens Grill Lounge?"

"I'll be there."

I'd no sooner hung up when the phone rang again.

"This is Jerry Lackman, Mrs. Fletcher."

"The famous detective, Billy Bravo. Good morning."

"I read about the play. Nobody told me there was going to be an added performance."

"You don't mind, do you? It'll be a reading. I've already talked to Rip about it. We're meeting for breakfast to discuss it."

"What's the play about?"

"I thought the insert in today's activity program spelled it out."

"It sure does. You wrote it based on Marla Tralaine's murder."

"Loosely based upon it."

"What part do I play?"

"One with which you're obviously comfortable—a detective called in to solve her murder, just as Billy Bravo does in the other play."

There was a long silence on his end; I could hear his mental gears turning.

"Maybe you and I should have a little talk. *Before* the play."

"Maybe we should. Ten?"

"Someplace we can be alone. How about the Crystal Bar? Nobody drinking there at that hour. It's on the Upper Deck Forward."

"I'll be there."

I hung up. The phone rang once more. It was journalist James Brady.

"Don't tell me," he said. "You've solved Marla Tralaine's murder."

"Far from it, Jim. But I do have a few ideas."

"And you're about to reveal those ideas in this play you've written."

"I just thought the other passengers would enjoy . . . would appreciate having a little light shed on a murder of a famous person that took place during their five days on the *QE2*."

"Oh, I'm sure they will. Care to give me a sneak preview of the play? I'm doing my satellite feed at noon."

"I'm sure you know as much as I do, Jim. The play is based upon supposition, nothing more."

"Come on, Jess. I know you better than that. It's okay if you want to play it close to the vest. But maybe I can give you a few lines to add."

"Oh?"

"Marla was strangled."

"Where did you hear that?"

"A reliable source. Here's another new line for you. Your director, Rip Nestor, has an interesting family background."

I held my breath. Had he learned that Rip was Marla Tralaine's son?

That's exactly what he then told me.

"I'd heard rumors," I said.

"What about his father?" Brady asked.

"You tell me. You seem to be tapped in to the right sources."

"Haven't pinned that down yet. You'll let me know if you do, of course."

"Of course."

The fact was I did have an idea of who Rip Nestor's father was, based upon input from Mary Ward. She didn't know for sure, of course. But her reasoning, coupled with an uncanny ability to see physical similarities in people, was compelling.

The question was, should I share it with my old friend James Brady? He'd been forthcoming with me. But I couldn't have him broadcast to the world what would be revealed in the play three hours later.

"Jim," I said, "if I tell you who I *think* Rip Nestor's father is—and I stress the word 'think'—will you promise not to broadcast it until after the play this afternoon?"

"Sure."

Had it been another journalist, I would not have

taken such a chance. But Brady had never gone back on his word with me before.

I told him.

His response was to whistle into the phone.

"I'm dealing with a hunch," I said. "Strictly a hunch."

"I understand. Mind if I call my producer in New York and suggest I do a second feed later today? After your play?"

"I don't have any problem with that."

"Great. Thanks, Jess. I'll be in the audience."

My announcement that a new one-act play, based upon Marla Tralaine's murder, would be performed that afternoon generated interest beyond those who called me that morning. It seemed everyone on the *QE2* was talking about it. I was approached by other passengers everywhere I went, including one passenger who chastised me for "cashing in" on tragedy. I didn't bother to explain that I wasn't seeking money or notoriety. I simply smiled and said I was sorry he felt that way. What else could I say?

My instinct after meeting with Jerry Lackman was to retreat to my cabin until it was time for the plays to be performed, and have lunch sent in. But I decided I might as well maintain a public posture. Bringing everything into the open was the reason for writing the one-act play in the first place. No sense playing the shrinking violet at this juncture.

The Queens Grill was abuzz with talk about my announcement in the program. My tablemates during lunch were now reduced to three—Judge Dan Solon, chef Carlo Di Giovanni, and Mary Ward. Elaine Ananthous would remain in her cabin for the rest of the crossing, we were told, under heavy sedation ordered by the ship's medical director. She'd been told by Mr. Prall that all indications were that Troy Radcliff had, indeed, taken his life by leaping into the sea, although he did not tell her about the videotape that confirmed Radcliff was dead.

With Elaine no longer taking meals in the dining room, Di Giovanni felt comfortable enough to abandon his self-imposed exile and to join us once again. I hadn't told him that Mary's illness was the result of Elaine having tampered with the mushrooms. There was enough bad blood between them to add more. I simply said that a chemical had evidently gotten onto the mushrooms. "Not your fault," I said. "Nothing to do with you."

We left the restaurant a few minutes before two and walked to the Grand Lounge, where Act Three of the murder mystery was about to begin. It was standing room only. The crowd spilled out into the broad hallways on either side. Passengers lined up three deep on the Grand Promenade, the front row hanging over the railing.

"My goodness," I said to Priscilla Warren, who'd joined us. "There's not enough room for everyone."

"Most of them are here because of what's to follow," she said.

"Thanks for getting the printing and photocopying done," I said. "Sorry to have woken you up out of a deep sleep."

"Happens on a regular basis," she said.

Rip Nestor stepped to the microphone, welcomed everyone, and recapped what had taken place in Acts One and Two. He introduced Detective Billy Bravo, played by Jerry Lackman, and the third act was under way.

The audience continued to grow, and seemed to enjoy this act as much as they had the first two. Lackman was impressive in the way he engaged audience members, cracking jokes about what he knew of their personal lives and identifying some of them as suspects.

The act ended a little before three. On the previous two days passengers quickly dispersed when the performance was over. Not today. No one made a move to leave.

"Looks like I'm on," I said, getting up from the table and heading for the stage, accompanied by Priscilla, who carried the dozen copies of the new script.

The actors and actresses had gathered behind screens, out of sight of the audience. Rip Nestor was with them.

"Everyone ready for the reading?" I asked.

"They're ready," Nestor said.

"Splendid. Priscilla, would you please pass out the scripts?" I'd marked each one with the character's name, and with the name of the actor or actress who'd play that person.

"I love readings," the young actress assigned to play Sam Teller's wife, Lila Sims, said. Her character's name was "Suzie Starlet."

I'd assigned names to the characters that would help the audience identify their roles.

Sam Teller was "Stan Mogul."

Peter Kunz was "Bob Manager."

Marla Tralaine's personal trainer was "Sal Biceps."

Troy Radcliff was named "Roy Climber."

Ms. Tralaine's hairdresser, Candy Malone, was "Cindy Curl."

Sydney Worrell, the gentleman host and actor with Marla Tralaine in *Dangerous Woman*, was "Dan Dancer."

Marla's lover when her husband was killed, Ron Ryan, was "Joe Gigolo."

The only character remaining the same from the other murder mystery play was Detective "Billy Bravo," played by Jerry Lackman.

"Ready, Rip?" I asked.

"I suppose so."

The cast sat in a semicircle on the stage. Nestor went to the microphone, surveyed the overflow crowd, cleared his voice, and read from the script: "You're about to be treated to a special one-act play written by the mystery writer, Jessica Fletcher. It's a work of fiction. But it *is* based on certain events that have taken place during this crossing on the *QE2*."

272

He went on to talk of Marla Tralaine's murder, where she'd been found, and of the speculation over who might have done such a dastardly deed.

"But this is fiction," he said, "and so we will not refer to the decreased actress as Marla Tralaine. For the purposes of this play, our murdered star is 'Veronica Rivers'."

The audience laughed. I wanted them to. I'd written the play as a broad farce, with heroes and villains to be cheered and booed.

"Fortunately for everyone, one of the world's great detectives, Billy Bravo, a legend in someone else's time, is also aboard. He's been called upon to investigate the brutal murder of Veronica Rivers. Let's see what he's come up with. Here he is—the Columbo of the high seas, the Sherlock Holmes of the North Atlantic, Billy Bravo!"

The crowd went wild, applauding and whistling and stamping their feet as Lackman stood and took a bow. Nestor stepped back, and Lackman took over, utilizing a wireless body mike.

"So what do we have here?" he asked, raising his eyebrows and wiggling his fingers in front of his mouth, as though holding a cigar. "We have a former famous movie actress, Veronica Rivers, attempting to make a comeback but having it thwarted by m-u-r-d-e-r."

"Go get 'em, Billy," a man yelled.

Lackman smiled and said, "That is exactly what I intend to do—with your help."

"We're with you, Billy," shouted a woman.

Applause.

"I've taken a close look at all the circumstances surrounding this brutal, wanton act, and I have some questions to ask those close to the deceased—v-e-r-y probing questions."

He spun around and faced the rest of the cast, seated behind him. "One of *you* snuffed out the life of Veronica Rivers. And I, Billy Bravo, sleuth without peer, intend to find out *who.*"

The cast looked at each other suspiciously, as the script directed them to do.

Lackman faced the audience again. "Let's see," he said. "What do we already know? We know that Veronica Rivers was found dead in a lifeboat on the Boat Deck, her naked, lifeless body discovered by another passenger taking a morning constitutional."

He cocked his head, waiting for audience reaction.

"Naked!" he shouted. "Why would she have been naked at the time of her death?" He lowered his voice. "Because she was taking a shower at the moment someone attacked her?"

"Nooooo," came a chorus from the audience.

"Ah ha," Lackman said. "I have an intuitive audience. No, my friends, she was not taking a shower. She was engaged in—hanky-panky!"

"Yesssss," said the onlookers.

"Is that what you call it?" a man asked loudly.

"Keep it clean," Lackman said. "This is a family show."

Much laughter.

From my vantage point backstage, I could see most of the Grand Lounge. Peter Kunz, Marla Tralaine's manager, sat at a table near the front with Lila Sims and Tony Silvestrie, Marla's personal fitness trainer. Ms. Sims attempted to be incognito; she wore oversized sunglasses and a large, floppy straw hat angled low over her eyes.

Interesting, I thought. While the play had enticed Sam Teller out of seclusion in his penthouse, he was not with his wife. He stood alone at the rear of the Grand Lounge, arms crossed defiantly on his chest, a scowl on his face.

Also standing, but at the opposite side of the room, was Sydney Worrell, the gentleman host who'd been in *Dangerous Woman* with Marla Tralaine.

Lackman now started interrogating the other cast members, weaving in clues I'd written into the script.

To "Sal Biceps": "You were Veronica Rivers's personal trainer."

"That's right," the actor playing him responded. "So what?"

"So what?" Lackman mocked. "So what? I'll tell you so what. You were supposed to be loyal to Ms. Rivers, but you seem to have a greater loyalty to a younger actress aboard the *QE2*. Yes, indeed. Judging from what I've observed, your allegiance is to Ms. Starlet—Miss Suzie Starlet, the aspiring young actress."

"You're crazy," Biceps said, waving away the suggestion and looking disgusted.

"But Ms. Starlet is a married woman," Lackman said.

"Big deal," Biceps said.

"Oh, but it *is* a big deal, Mr. Sal Biceps. It is a big deal because Suzie Starlet's husband happens to be the head of a large and powerful television network, Mr. Stan Mogul."

Sal Biceps looked down at the floor.

"A dangerous move, Mr. Biceps, considering you've been angling for your own aerobics television show on Mogul's network."

The actress playing Lila Sims—"Suzie Starlet"—got up from her chair, as directed to do in the script, and started walking away.

"Hold on there, Ms. Starlet. Not so fast."

She turned and opened her eyes with exaggerated surprise. "Yes?" she asked demurely.

"You've had some pretty stiff competition for your husband's affections, haven't you, you pretty young thing."

"I don't know what you're talking about," she said, pouting.

"I suggest you sit down," Lackman said, "and I'll explain it to you."

She returned to her chair.

Lackman now turned his attention to Peter Kunz—"Bob Manager."

"You, sir, are an ambitious young man."

The actor smiled smugly. "Nothing wrong with ambition, is there?"

"Not unless it leads to—murder!"

The actor playing Bob Manager jumped to his feet. "Now, wait a minute," he snarled. "Are you suggesting that—?"

"Sit down!" Lackman yelled.

"You tell 'em, Billy," an audience member said.

The crowd started to chant, "Billy, Billy, Billy."

Lackman stepped to the stage apron and held up his hands. "Please, please," he said. "I know I deserve your adoration, but save it for when I solve the case."

Applause followed him back to where he resumed questioning "Bob Manager."

"You were Ms. Rivers's manager, negotiating a two-movie contract with Stan Mogul, head of the network."

"That's right."

"Yet the moment your boss, Ms. Rivers, was killed, you began negotiating on your own behalf."

"No crime in that."

"But not very sensitive."

"This is business. There's no room for sensitivity in business."

"Alas, how true," Lackman said, bringing his hands to his bosom and delivering the line in Shakespearean fashion. "But that doesn't mean murder has a place in the boardroom."

"I didn't kill anybody," Manager said.

"That remains to be seen," said Lackman.

Ron Ryan, the older actor who'd been Marla Tralaine's lover years ago, played himself under the character name "Joe Gigolo." He didn't know it, of course, because he hadn't seen the script until just moments before the performance. Now, as Billy Bravo addressed him, he realized what was going on, but couldn't do anything about it short of leaving, which would have been awkward.

"Joe Gigolo," Lackman said slowly, as though chewing on the name. "We go back a long way."

"We do?"

"Oh, yes, we certainly do."

Although Jerry Lackman also hadn't seen the script prior to the performance, he knew where it was heading because I'd told him during our meeting that morning.

At first, he'd denied my accusation that he'd been one of the LAPD detectives who'd investigated the murder of Marla Tralaine's husband years ago. But he eventually admitted I was right. I asked him during that meeting why he was on this crossing. "It has to be more than just wanting an acting job," I'd said.

Not only did he agree with me, he told me the real reason for signing on with Rip Nestor. It wasn't what

Mary Ward and I had speculated; it was even more revealing and meaningful.

"You and Veronica Rivers were close friends, weren't you, Mr. Gigolo?" Lackman asked.

"I . . ."

"*Much* more than good friends. You were lovers once."

"Yes, we were." Ryan said the line as though being tortured with cattle prods.

"And you were close to her late husband, too."

"I knew him."

I had the feeling Ryan might bolt from the stage.

"He owed you a lot of money, didn't he?"

"I don't have to answer your questions," Ryan said. That line wasn't in the script.

"But you will."

Ryan started to get up, but Lackman quickly placed his hand on the older actor's shoulder and kept him in his seat. He then spun around to confront the actor playing the gentleman host, Sydney Worrell, whom I'd renamed "Dan Dancer."

"You, Mr. Dancer, also have a relationship with the deceased that goes back a number of years."

"That is correct."

"You appeared with Ms. Rivers in one of her films, *Dangerous Woman*."

"Right again, Detective."

I looked out over the audience to where the real

Sydney Worrell continued to stand. Then I shifted my attention to the position where Sam Teller had been standing. He was gone. I shortened my focus. Lila Sims, Tony Silvestrie, and Peter Kunz were still at the front table.

"You were in love with Veronica Rivers, weren't you, Mr. Dancer?"

"Yes. Deeply in love."

"And you still are!"

The actor raised his chin. "Yes. I have loved her from the first day we met on the set."

"But she spurned you," said Lackman. "For all these years you've carried a torch for her that was not reciprocated. And when you sent up a note to her penthouse on this crossing, she ignored it—ignored *you*."

"She—"

"Enough!" Lackman snapped. "It's time for Billy Bravo to solve the murder of Veronica Rivers."

The audience erupted in applause and cheering.

"First," Lackman said, "let me review what we know. We know that Veronica Rivers was found naked, and dead in the lifeboat."

"Go get 'em, Billy," an audience member offered.

"Go, Billy, go! Go, Billy, go!"

"Second, we have agreed that she was in her birthday suit because she was interrupted by her murderer while engaging in—hanky-panky!"

"Right on, Billy," a woman shouted.

"Now," Lackman continued, "who might have been

her partner in hanky-panky?" He asked various members of the audience for their suggestions. They were many and varied, including every male character.

"It's my contention that Veronica Rivers was killed because she played hanky-panky with the wrong man," Lackman continued. "We have to decide which partner in hanky-panky would be someone who would make someone else mad—mad enough to murder."

Again, suggestions flew from the audience.

"The men sitting up here would not fall into that category. Who would care whether Bob Manager, Sal Biceps, Joe Gigolo, or Dan Dancer played hanky-panky with Veronica Rivers? No one!"

"What about him?" a man shouted, pointing to the actor playing Troy Radcliff, a.k.a "Roy Climber."

Lackman faced Climber. "What about you, Mr. Climber?"

The actor said in a deep baritone, "I didn't play hanky-panky with Veronica Rivers. Besides, no one would care if I did. She wasn't married—anymore."

"True," said Lackman, following the script. "That no one would care. But you did have an intimate relationship with Veronica Rivers."

Roy Climber gave out a theatrical sigh and sat back.

"Which leaves," Lackman said, "only you, Mr. Stan Mogul."

The actor playing Mogul displayed a smug smile, saying nothing.

"Only you would have upset someone by playing hanky-panky with Veronica Rivers." Lackman shot the audience a knowing smile. "Because you have a young wife who would be v-e-r-y upset finding you in a compromising position with your former lover."

Stan Mogul jumped to his feet. "Are you suggesting that—?"

"I am not suggesting anything, Mr. Mogul," Lackman said. "I am saying without hesitation or reservation that Veronica Rivers was killed because of her sexual relationship with you."

Mogul started to say something else, but Lackman interrupted. "Not only that, sir, you were happy to see her dead because of the threat she held over you head."

Mogul, who'd sat again, guffawed. "What threat?"

"The threat of revealing that you and Veronica Rivers had a son together, a son neither of you have acknowledged. Veronica threatened to reveal that the young man was the result of a union between the two of you many years ago."

"Let's say everything you say is true," Mogul said. "But that doesn't prove I killed her."

"No, it doesn't," Lackman said. "But you know who did."

A silence fell over the large crowd.

Lackman surveyed them with raised eyebrows. No doubt about it, he was a wonderful actor, completely in control of his role and his audience.

"Excuse me," Suzie Starlet said, standing. "I have somewhere else I must be."

Lackman spun around. "Getting hot in here, Ms. Starlet?"

I looked to the table where Lila Sims, Tony Silvestrie, and Peter Kunz had been sitting. Ms. Sims abruptly stood. Mary Ward, who sat at an adjacent table, also stood.

I watched Sims snake her way through the tables and head for the hallway. To my amazement, Mary Ward followed.

"Mary," I said in a voice loud enough for her to hear.

"What?" Lackman said, looking at me.

Mary started to pass the table where Lila Sims had been sitting, but Tony Silvestrie stood and blocked her way.

Mary looked up at him and said, "You are a very rude young man."

Lackman realized what was happening and barked into the microphone, "Ms. Sims. Please don't leave."

The crowded room had made it difficult for her to reach the hallway. She stopped at the sound of her name, turned, and looked at Lackman.

"Please, sit down, Ms. Sims," Lackman said, forcing charm into his voice. "The play isn't over yet."

Mary Ward had almost reached Sims. There was a hush in the audience. Mary said, "Why not stay, dear?

Mrs. Fletcher has worked hard on the play. It's impolite to leave before it's over."

I suppressed a smile. Lila Sims didn't seem to know what to do. She looked to where Silvestrie and Kunz stood at their table. They, too, appeared confused. Every eye in the audience was on Sims. Slowly, she threaded through the crowd and returned to her table. So did Mary.

Lackman said, "Good. Now I can get back to solving this unfortunate, *fictitious* murder. Where was I? Oh, yes. I was saying that Veronica Rivers was killed because she'd engaged in hanky-panky with Stan Mogul. Mr. Mogul's young wife, Suzie Starlet, discovered them together. Must have been a shock, a real kick to her ego."

"She did it!" an audience member shouted. "Suzie Starlet."

"No, she didn't," Lackman said, returning to the script.

"How do you know?" another person in the crowd asked.

"Two reasons," Lackman said. "I admit it taxed my superior deductive powers. But as usual, I overcame all obstacles. Suzie Starlet couldn't have done it because she doesn't have the strength. Veronica Rivers was strangled. And her body was removed to the lifeboat." He turned to Starlet. "This little wisp of a woman couldn't have done either."

"She had an accomplice," the audience offered.

"Exactly!" said Lackman.

"Who was it, Billy?"

I looked around for Rip Nestor. He'd been standing next to me throughout the play. He no longer was.

"The hardest part for me was coming up with Suzie Starlet's accomplice in murder," Lackman said, still consulting the script, but ad-libbing his way through it. "I have to admit that even the great Billy Bravo was stymied for a while. But *only* for a while."

He turned to Roy Climber, in real life mountain climber Troy Radcliff. "You, Mr. Climber, gave me my answer."

"Me? How could I have done that?"

"By giving your life."

The audience gasped.

Lackman continued: "You see, ladies and gentlemen, Mr. Climber, despite his advanced age, continued to enjoy intimacy with beautiful women. Unfortunately, this penchant for female companionship caused him . . ." He spun around and directly faced the actor playing Climber. ". . . caused *you* to be in the wrong place at the wrong time."

All attention focused on Climber.

A literal-minded member of the audience yelled, "How come he's sitting there if he died?"

"Aha," said Lackman, finger pointed in the air. "An excellent question. In the interest of theater, it was necessary to resurrect Mr. Climber for purposes of this performance. The truth is, Mr. Climber did, indeed, give his life—and in doing so, he has given us the answer to that perplexing question of who killed Veronica Rivers, at Ms. Suzie Starlet's behest."

"Who?" a dozen voices asked.

"Elementary, my dear audience. The answer is captured on videotape. You see, the excellent crew of this magnificent vessel saw fit to install a video surveillance camera at the precise spot where Mr. Climber lost his life."

"They did?" The question was asked loudly by Sal Biceps.

I looked to the table where Tony Silvestrie sat with Sims and Kunz. The physical fitness trainer reacted like a trapped animal. He stood. So did Lila Sims.

"Shall we, as they say, roll the tape?" Lackman asked. "It's quite revealing. Mr. Climber had to be eliminated because he knew who'd killed Veronica Rivers." To Mogul: "Did he threaten to tell the authorities, Mr. Mogul?"

Silvestrie and Sims pushed people out of their way and headed for an exit. The actor and actress playing them also stood and began arguing. The audience didn't know who to watch, the departing real-life duo, or the actor and actress on stage.

Lackman said, "So, my devoted fans, the murder is solved. Stan Mogul was caught in the act of hanky-panky with Veronica Rivers by his nubile wife, the lovely Suzie Starlet. She enlisted the aid of Ms. Rivers's personal trainer, Sal Biceps, in strangling Rivers and removing her naked body to a lifeboat on the Boat Deck, where she was discovered by a health-conscious passenger walking off a big breakfast."

Stan Mogul proclaimed, "That's right. That's the way it happened."

Lackman confronted him on-stage. "But you knew all about it, Mr. Mogul. In fact, you condoned it, were relieved that your lover was now out of the way."

"Why would I feel that way?" Mogul asked.

"Because Veronica Rivers was blackmailing you into starring her in movies for your cable network. And what did she have to hold over your head?"

"Yeah! What was it?" the audience asked.

"That son born to Veronica Rivers and you many years ago. A son that you, Stan Mogul, refused to acknowledge as your own."

I looked at James Brady, who sat at a table in the middle of the room, making notes. He glanced at me, smiled, made the okay sign with his fingers, and resumed writing.

Mary Ward smiled and nodded smugly. She seemed extremely satisfied.

But the play wasn't over.

Lackman picked up where he'd left off, directing his next comments at Joe Manager. "You, Mr. Manager, were also happy to see your boss, Veronica Rivers, dead."

The actor replied, "Why should I be?"

"Because it gave you leverage with Mr. Mogul. You

now knew that his wife, Suzie Starlet, and Ms. Rivers's physical fitness trainer, Sal Biceps, had killed Rivers. And that makes *you* an accomplice to murder."

Everyone waited for Bob Manager to deliver his line from the script.

Instead, the answer came from Peter Kunz, seated alone at the table formerly occupied by him, Lila Sims, and Tony Silvestrie. "I tried to stop them, damn it, but they wouldn't listen."

"He's in the play?" a wife asked her husband.

"Who's he?" someone else asked.

Kunz stood. "I'm not taking the rap for anybody." With that, he almost knocked over audience members, toppled two chairs, and ran from the Grand Lounge to the loud boos of the audience, which still assumed he was part of the show.

Security Chief Wallace Prall, who'd been standing at the foot of the stage, leaped up to where I stood. "If I read this right, Mrs. Fletcher, the play reflects what *really* happened to Marla Tralaine."

"Yes, it does," I said. "Thanks to that lady there." I pointed to Mary Ward.

"We don't have any arrest powers," he said, "unless passenger safety is in jeopardy."

"I don't think that's a problem, Mr. Prall. No one can go anywhere until we reach Southampton. I would suggest that Mr. Kunz be provided round-the-clock security, and be segregated from others. He's obviously willing to talk, which will help turn speculation into hard evidence."

"I'll take care of that right away."

"I'm glad we didn't have to show the videotape of Mr. Radcliff being tossed overboard by Mr. Silvestrie."

"I am, too."

"Any word on Scotland Yard flying in?" I asked.

"It looked this morning as though the weather would delay that. But we're out of the storm. Captain Marwick says it's clear sailing in sunshine right into Southampton."

"How symbolic," I said. "Will you excuse me?"

"Of course."

I joined Mary Ward at the table.

"That was wonderful, Jessica," she said. "I truly enjoyed it."

"So did I—in a strange way."

"What will you do for the rest of the day?"

"Start enjoying this ship, and the short time we have left on it. Besides, I have a special friend who'll be arriving by helicopter any minute."

Chapter Twenty-five

Captain Marwick hosted a private cocktail party that evening for the Scotland Yard team, led by George Sutherland. The captain's surprisingly large and handsomely furnished and appointed apartment was the perfect setting for the intimate gathering.

Besides George and his four-person team, and me, there was Mary Ward, Rip Nestor, James Brady, Jerry Lackman, Pamela Fiori and Michael Cannon of *Town and Country*, the British journalists, and a few other specially invited guests. The captain, looking splendid in his dress-whites, and his beautiful wife were the perfect host and hostess, roles in which they'd obviously found themselves countless times.

It lasted an hour. Following it, George and I escaped to a quiet corner of the Chart House Bar.

"Your arrival couldn't have been better timed," I said after our waitress had put down a dark ale for him and a glass of white wine for me.

"Let's toast to that," he said in his deep voice, tinged with the Scottish brogue of his ancestry.

"I told the security director that there wasn't a problem because no one could leave the ship. But I feel a lot more comfortable having Sam Teller and his crew in your custody."

"I share your feelings. You might have been in jeopardy had they been free to roam the ship. That young fellow, Kunz, is the sort of man I dislike intensely," George said. "No backbone, no character."

"But helpful to have someone like that around in times like this," I said. "He's corroborated everything Mrs. Ward and I conjured in the play."

"Yes, it is handy having a spineless member of a criminal group to tell all. This actor, Lackman, intrigues me. A former member of the Los Angeles detective squad turned private investigator—and actor."

"We had trouble figuring him out, George, until I cornered him and wrung it out of him."

George laughed. "I've seen you at work before, Jessica. You're a born interrogator."

"Actually, it wasn't that difficult. Once I knew— once Mary Ward and I knew—he'd been one of the detectives investigating the murder of Marla Tralaine's husband years ago, it just made sense to assume he wasn't on the ship only as an actor in the theatrical troupe. But I was surprised he'd been hired by Sam Teller to build a case against Marla Tralaine as having murdered her husband. According to Lackman, Teller wanted that in his pocket as a tool in negotiating with her. His failing was his inability to keep his libido in check. If he hadn't ..." I laughed. "If he hadn't engaged in *hanky-panky* with her, things would have turned out different. What a wonderful term that is. Mary Ward came up with it to, as she put it, 'present sexual indiscretions in a more genteel manner.' "

"Quite a lady."

"Certainly is. I've never met anyone quite like her. She picked up on every subtlety, every nuance, and created a scenario that proved to be true."

"Back to Lackman," George said, sipping his ale. "You say he signed on with this Teller fellow to build a case against the actress."

"Yes. That's one murder that will never be solved."

"What happened once she was killed?"

"He decided to retreat from Teller, finish the crossing as an actor, and forget about it. But when he tried to get paid by Teller, and Teller balked, Jerry became angry. Once I told him of what we suspected in Tralaine's murder, he was more than happy to cooperate. He's wonderful on stage, George. A real talent."

"I'd like to see him in action."

"You can. The final act of the play—the original play I wrote—is tomorrow afternoon."

"But I have to fly back in the morning."

"Can't you stay until we reach Southampton? It's only an extra day."

"I suppose I could. The other chaps can take Mr. Teller and his crew back themselves."

"Will you? Stay?"

"Yes. I think I shall."

"Wonderful."

"Shame about that mountain climber, Radcliff. I'd seen his show on the telly back home. Amazing specimen for his age."

"I thought he'd taken his life because of the terminal illness he had. Not the sort of man to do that, though. According to Peter Kunz, Radcliff had been with Marla when Teller said he wanted to see her. Radcliff tried to leave, but Teller was at her door too fast, so he hid in one of the huge closets in her penthouse. He was there when Teller virtually raped Marla, and when Lila Sims burst in. Must have been quite a scene. Silvestrie and Kunz heard the commotion and followed Lila into the penthouse. Kunz says Silvestrie hated Marla, and attacked her without provocation by Lila Sims. But you say that Silvestrie told you during your initial interrogation that Lila told him to kill her."

"That's right. He said Lila screamed, 'Get rid of the bitch.' And he did."

"She had considerable power over him."

"More a case of his wanting his own television show. He evidently figured Ms. Sims and her husband would return the favor."

"Quite a collection of bad people."

"Unsavory lot, that's for certain."

George ordered a second ale.

"Initially, Mary and I thought the gentleman host on the ship, Mr. Worrell, or Tralaine's former lover, Ron Ryan, might have been involved. Turned out not to be true."

"Fortunate for them. They're both too old to end up in prison for the rest of their lives. What about Mr. Nestor, your director? You say he is the illegitimate son of Tralaine and Sam Teller."

"That's right. I feel sorry for him, coming from that background. But he actually seems relieved now that it's all come out into the open. Even agreed to be interviewed by James Brady on his TV satellite feed this afternoon. Maybe he can turn it to his professional advantage."

"That would be good. Well, Jessica, what does the rest of the evening hold in store for us?"

"Dinner in the Queens Grill. You haven't met the TV chef, Carlo Di Giovanni, or Judge Solon. I doubt whether Elaine Ananthous will show up for meals."

"Who is she?"

"The TV plant lady. Odd bird. Had a long-term relationship with Troy Radcliff. A pathetic woman, but decent enough, I suppose."

"And after dinner?"

"Up to dancing? The ship's orchestra is wonderful."

"Not my strength."

"You're too modest. We've danced together before."

"Yes, we have. I'll give it my best."

"And then—well, there's so much to do and see on the ship. Tomorrow's tea dance is a must. The Tommy Dorsey Orchestra plays every afternoon. There's the spa and the sports deck. And, of course, the final act of my play. But do you know what I most want to share with you?

"Tell me."

"To be wrapped in blankets on the top deck and be served hot bouillon. That's eleven in the morning. Somehow, it represents for me what crossing the North Atlantic is really all about—the ultimate decadent, luxurious experience."

He grinned and finished his ale. "It's good to see you, Jessica."

"Aren't you going to add 'under such unfortunate circumstances?' "

"I'll take seeing Jessica Fletcher under any circumstances. Come on. If this clumsy Scotsman is going to do something as adventurous as dancing, he'll need a good meal under his belt."

I flew home from London on the British Airways Concorde, an exciting way to end my British holiday. I lost track of Mary Ward while in London, but received a long letter from her a few days after arriving back in Cabot Cove. Her family loved the gifts she'd brought; she said she had settled in again nicely in Lumberton, North Carolina, busy with a variety of pursuits, including doing her crossword puzzles and, of course, devouring murder mysteries and solving them before the authors intended.

Her closing line was:

> If you plan to take the *QE2* to England again next year, Jessica, I hope you'll let me know in plenty of time for me to make a reservation. Being on this crossing with you was such fun, I'd hate to miss another opportunity .
>
> Fondly, Mary

I put her letter in a desk drawer, picked up the phone, and called my travel agent, Susan Shevlin.

"Dying to hear all about the trip," she said.

"I'll stop by tomorrow," I said. "In the meantime, would you book me again on the *QE2* for next May? The twenty-eighth, if possible."

"Really loved it, huh, despite the murder?"

"Yes. Really loved it. See you tomorrow."

I pulled out a piece of fancy stationery, thought for a moment, then wrote: "Dear Mary, I just spoke to my travel agent and . . ."

Voyage to Russia in the next
Murder, She Wrote mystery novel
Murder in Moscow,
coming from Signet in 1998.

The flight from Washington to Moscow had been long and tiring, and I was delighted to finally be in my suite in the opulent Palace Hotel, at the upper end of Tverskaya, a prime and convenient location. My perception of accommodations in Russia was that I shouldn't expect much in the way of service and amenities. My perception turned out to be faulty.

The spacious and handsome suite was on two levels. There were two bedrooms and two full baths upstairs, and a dining and living room on the lower level. The furnishings were light pine, giving the rooms a pleasant open feel. Most striking was the art and sculpture. It was like staying in a mini-museum.

I unpacked, hung up my clothes, and explored the rooms. Management had provided a platter of cheeses, fruit, a small dish of caviar nestled in crushed ice, tiny shrimp, and a bottle of champagne. I opened a small envelope tucked between two apples: "Welcome, Mrs. Fletcher, to the Palace Hotel and to Moscow.

We stand ready to meet your every need." It was signed by the hotel's assistant manager.

My fatigue was now replaced by a sense of excitement and energy. The actuality that I was, indeed, in Moscow suddenly hit me. I experienced what the great psychologist Abraham Maslow termed a "peak experience." And that led me to realize, as I often do, that I was a very fortunate person living a blessed life.

I'd changed my watch to Russian time before leaving Washington, and saw that I had two hours before we were to gather in the hotel's dining room for our first meal together on Russian soil. By now, we'd gotten to know each other pretty well. The Russian publishing executives who'd traveled to Washington at the invitation of our Commerce Department were a gregarious lot; dinners and cocktail parties were spirited and loud. One gentleman in particular, Vladislav Staritova, who'd purchased the Russian publishing rights to my most recent murder mystery before leaving Moscow for the Washington conference, was especially friendly. He spoke excellent English, and we spent many hours discussing my book, his company, and how Russia could develop a prosperous publishing industry during the difficult transition years ahead. My only difficulty with him was that after he'd consumed enough vodka, he became comically amorous. It was at those times I felt a sudden need to "powder my nose," as the saying goes.

When I arrived at the hotel's large banquet room, I

was surprised to see that the number of people for dinner had swelled to more than double what it had been in Washington. Wives of the Russian executives had joined us, as well as a dozen or so men who I assumed were employees of the publishing houses represented. The male newcomers were a sullen lot, so unlike their bosses. They tended to stay to themselves, huddled in groups of two and three away from the main group at the cocktail party. As had been true in Washington, the vodka and champagne flowed freely, as did a dazzling array of hors d'oeuvres on large silver trays proudly carried by uniformed waiters.

"Nicely settled in your room?" asked Sam Roberts, the Commerce Department official responsible for the exchange project between American and Russian publishers.

"Room? It's a magnificent suite," I said.

"Glad you're happy, Jessica. I must tell you that including you in the group was one of my smarter moves."

"Oh?"

"You've absolutely charmed the Russians."

"I'm enjoying their company."

"They're all intrigued that you write murder mysteries."

"A universal fascination, I suppose," I replied. "Like American jazz. A common language. Everyone loves a good mystery to solve."

Roberts, an angular man with close-cropped, salt-and-pepper hair and a ready smile, said, "Well, enjoy dinner and the rest of your stay in Russia. We've tried to leave enough time for you and the others to do a bit of sightseeing."

"And I intend to take full advantage of that."

The tables for dinner were arranged in a horseshoe. I found myself seated between Vladislav Staritova, my new Russian publisher, and one of the younger men who was new to our group. I introduced myself to him and received a grunt and weak handshake in return. The stereotype of the brooding Russian came to mind, but I silently reminded myself that it was probably more a problem of generational than national origins. Young people in America seem to have become more sullen and morose, too, these days. Why? I have no idea.

As the food started arriving from the kitchen, I thought of what my friend back in Cabot Cove had said when she learned I'd be coming to Russia: "The Russians have the most fattening diet in the world. They take in seventy percent more calories a day than we do."

I certainly wouldn't debate her now that my first Russian dinner was being served. It started with caviar, *ikra* in Russian, proceeded to a large bowl of borscht, then featured a salad of tomatoes and cucumbers (I'd been told Russians don't use lettuce), and went on to such dishes as *zhulienn*, a casserole of mushrooms and sour cream, and the main course, *tsiplyonok*, chicken smothered with a rich, heavy cream sauce.

Dessert would be *rizhok*, a layered pastry with chocolate sauce and whipped cream. All of it, of course, accompanied by a river of vodka and champagne.

The main course was about to be served when our official Russian host, a corpulent gentleman who held a similar position in his government as Sam Roberts did with the American Commerce Department, stood and welcomed everyone in flawless English, tossing in an occasional translation for those Russians who weren't bilingual. He talked for a long time, which held up the waiters, and concluded his remarks by introducing Sam Roberts. Roberts also spoke too long as far as I was concerned—a disease infecting all politicians. As he did, my mind wandered, and I took in others at the tables. The younger men, who'd remained aloof during the cocktail party, were scattered among the other dinner guests. The drink and food hadn't lightened their spirits. They still carried those brooding, bordering-on-angry expressions. I'd tried to engage my adjacent tablemate in conversation, but never got very far. It wasn't a language barrier. From what little he said, he spoke a fair amount of English.

Sam Roberts concluded his remarks, and the waiters got on with the job of delivering the main course to the tables. Vladislav Staritova had consumed a lot of vodka. His speech was slightly slurred, and he'd reverted to directing terms of endearment to me, despite the presence of his wife at his immediate right.

"Ah, my favorite," he said, looking at the chicken that had just been placed before him, rubbing his hands and licking his lips. "You will like this very much, Jessica," he said. "A sweet meal for a sweet lady." He winked at me; the back of his hand brushed my thigh, and I moved my chair a few inches away.

I barely touched my entree; I was stuffed from all the rich food that had come before. The vodka and champagne had loosened everyone's tongue, and the noise level had steadily risen as dinner progressed.

A trio of Russian musicians started playing, which added to the festive spirit permeating the room. One of the Russian publishers insisted that the wife of an American join him on the dance floor in the center of the horseshoe table setup. The music had an infectious melody and beat, and we began clapping as the man and woman awkwardly moved to the music.

"Jessica?" Staritova said, pushing himself up and grabbing my hand.

"Oh, no," I said. "Absolutely not."

I heard his wife say, "Sit down, you old fool."

He did, to my relief.

His wife's harsh comment had deflated him. He sat dejectedly, eyes focused on his empty plate, mouth moving as though rehearsing a retort.

A waiter whisked away our plates, followed by another waiter who placed desserts in front of us. The pastries were smothered in chocolate sauce and whipped cream. The band played louder. Others joined the couple on the dance floor. I started to feel dizzy, and slightly nauseous.

I didn't know the name of the song, but it reached a point where the Russians suddenly yelped some phrase in concert with the musicians.

I considered leaving the table and going to a restroom. It had all been too much—the long flight, the trip from the airport into town, all the food and drink—although I'd barely sipped some vodka to be polite to my hosts—the music and noise and . . .

I turned to excuse myself to Staritova.

He looked at me. His eyes bulged, his mouth hung open. His face was beet red, the color of the borscht we'd had earlier.

"Are you all right?" I asked.

He replied by squaring himself in his chair, taking a deep and prolonged breath, and pitching forward, his face hitting his dessert plate with a thud. Chocolate syrup and whipped cream gushed from the plate, creating a black-and-white nest for his face.

His wife screamed.

No one heard because of the music and singing.

I turned to the dour young man at my left, but he was gone.

"Help!" I shouted, standing.

The music stopped. People turned and looked at me.

I pointed to Staritova.

"He's dead," I said.

And so he was.

Excerpt from *Murder in Moscow*

A sudden heart attack?

That certainly would have been preferable to what an overnight autopsy revealed. Vladislav Staritova, my Russian publisher, had been poisoned.